3 50

STANDOFF

The man stood up and spread his feet for balance on the steps. He was wearing his gun tied down. His friends scattered, not wanting to be near him, or especially behind him when the shooting started.

The man rubbed the bump on his head. "You ain't gonna surprise me today."

"You never know," Clint said.

They stared at each other for a moment, until Clint realized the man wanted him to make the first move. He wondered what would happen if he just stood there and waited, but he didn't have the time to waste.

"This is a bad reason to die, just to keep me from going inside," Clint said.

"That and the bump on my head are enough to kill you," the other man said.

"You can get over a bump," Clint said. "Hell, you can even get over being embarrassed in front of your friends . . ." Clint's eyes narrowed as he lowered his hand next to his pistol.

". . . But dead, that you aren't going to get over."

D0188263

DON'T MISS THESE
ALL-ACTION WESTERN SERIES
FROM THE BERKLEY PUBLISHING GROUP

THE GUNSMITH by J. R. Roberts
Clint Adams was a legend among lawmen, outlaws, and ladies.
They called him . . . the Gunsmith.

LONGARM by Tabor Evans
The popular long-running series about U.S. Deputy Marshal
Long—his life, his loves, his fight for justice.

SLOCUM by Jake Logan
Today's longest-running action Western. John Slocum rides
a deadly trail of hot blood and cold steel.

BUSHWHACKERS by B. J. Lanagan
An action-packed series by the creators of Longarm! The
rousing adventures of the most brutal gang of cutthroats ever
assembled—Quantrill's Raiders.

DIAMONDBACK by Guy Brewer
Dex Yancey is Diamondback, a southern gentleman turned
con man when his brother cheats him out of the family for-
tune. Ladies love him. Gamblers hate him. But nobody pulls
one over on Dex . . .

WILDGUN by Jack Hanson
Will Barlow's continuing search for his daughter, kidnapped
by the Blackfeet Indians who slaughtered the rest of his family.

THE GUNSMITH

236

THE CHEROKEE STRIP

J. R. ROBERTS

JOVE BOOKS, NEW YORK

If you purchased this book without a cover, you should be aware that this book is stolen property. It was reported as "unsold and destroyed" to the publisher and neither the author nor the publisher has received any payment for this "stripped book."

This is a work of fiction. Names, characters, places, and incidents are either the product of the author's imagination or are used fictitiously, and any resemblance to actual persons, living or dead, business establishments, events, or locales is entirely coincidental.

THE CHEROKEE STRIP

A Jove Book / published by arrangement with
the author

PRINTING HISTORY
Jove edition / August 2001

All rights reserved.
Copyright © 2001 by Robert J. Randisi.
This book, or parts thereof, may not be reproduced in any form
without permission.
For information address: The Berkley Publishing Group,
a division of Penguin Putnam Inc.,
375 Hudson Street, New York, New York 10014.

The Penguin Putnam Inc. World Wide Web site address is
www.penguinputnam.com

ISBN: 0-515-13118-0

A JOVE BOOK®
Jove Books are published by The Berkley Publishing Group,
a division of Penguin Putnam Inc.,
375 Hudson Street, New York, New York 10014.
JOVE and the "J" design
are trademarks belonging to Penguin Putnam Inc.

PRINTED IN THE UNITED STATES OF AMERICA

10 9 8 7 6 5 4 3 2 1

ONE

Clint Adams had been to Caldwell, Kansas, many times in his life. The very first time was when he was hunting buffalo with Wyatt Earp and Bat Masterson, all of them a lot younger than they were today. On occasion, over the years, he had run into a friend or two in Caldwell. This was the first time, however, that he'd ever come here when there was so much at stake for so many people.

Not that there was really anything at stake for him, personally, but he had a lot of friends who were working on negotiating a lease for 6.5 million acres of the Cherokee Outlet to be used by members of the newly formed Cherokee Strip Livestock Association. What he didn't understand was why there was an association before there was a lease.

He was here to help, but he had no idea what it was he was supposed to do. The man he was meeting was going to tell him that.

He rode to the livery and left Eclipse, his horse, there to be cared for, then came back to Main Street to check

1

into the Caldwell House Hotel. The streets were very crowded, as there were more people in Caldwell for the meetings then there were actual members of the association. The meetings with the Cherokee had been well ballyhooed and people were very curious to see what occurred.

Clint checked into the hotel at about three P.M. He was to meet with his friend Charley Pearlberg at the Cattlemen's Steak House at six. He had three hours to kill, so he decided to kill some of it with a bath and then a beer.

After his bath he picked one of the smaller saloons in town to have his beer in. While standing at the bar he listened to all of the talk going on around him about the leasing of the Cherokee Strip. The room seemed to be equally divided between those who favored it and those who were against it.

"We got no business offering the Cherokee money," one man opined. "We oughta go in there and take what we want."

"Start the Indian wars all over again, ya mean?" another man asked. "That's real smart."

"You callin' me stupid?"

"That's what I'm callin' ya."

Their friends intervened and got both men to have another beer instead of having a fight. Over the second beer they continued to give their opinions, and each man had their backers.

Clint checked the time. It was ten to six so he finished the rest of his beer, and left the saloon and its inhabitants to their argument.

• • •

The Cattleman's Steak House was in the Cattleman's Club, which was a three-story brick building that had been recently erected. There was a crowd gathered outside, but there didn't seem to be any purpose to their presence. They were just standing around, leaning against posts, sitting on the steps. As Clint approached he saw a man start to mount the steps to enter the building, but the men seated there would not move. The man faltered, then turned and walked away. Now he saw their purpose.

As he got closer he could see the seated men laughing and nudging each other. Apparently, there were people in town who were against paying the Cherokee for their land, who were willing to do something other than sit in a saloon and talk about it.

Clint reached the steps and started up. The men stuck their jaws out at him and didn't move. There were four of them, and others gathered around to watch.

"Excuse me," Clint said.

"Can't go in," one of them said.

"Why not?"

"You ain't a member." The spokesman was in his thirties, had his hat pushed back on his head and was leaning back on his elbows.

"How do you know?"

"I can tell."

"Well," Clint said, "as it happened I've been invited by a member, so if you'll just move aside—"

"Can't," the man said, cutting him off.

Clint knew his next logical step was to say. "Why?" again, but he decided to do something else. He reached down and grabbed the man by the back of his ankles and pulled. The man yelped and then the back of his head hit one of the steps as Clint dragged him out into the street and left him there. He then turned to go up the steps, but the other three had gotten to their feet. All were armed, but none of them looked ready to use their guns.

"Excuse me," Clint said to them.

They stared at him for a few seconds, then slowly parted, giving him a path up the steps.

"Thank you," he said, and stepped by them.

His instincts were on alert as he approached the door, in case any of them decided to make a move at his back. If that happened he wouldn't hesitate to kill anyone who tried it. He hated nothing on this earth more than a back-shooter.

He got to the door and stepped inside, then moved away from the line of sight outside. Only then did he release the breath he was holding. He'd be real happy if he didn't have to kill someone today.

TWO

Once inside Clint became the object of everyone's attentions. They'd been aware of what had been going on outside, and Clint was apparently the only man willing or able to run the blockade.

He was looking around for Charley Pearlberg when another man approached him. He was tall, gray-haired, barrel-chested, wearing an expensive three-piece suit and holding an expensive cigar.

"That was impressive," the man said.

"That?" Clint asked. "I just made a path for myself, is all."

"Well, that's more than anyone else has been willing to do for hours," the man said. He stuck his hand out. "My name's Mathis, Ed Mathis."

"Adams," Clint said, shaking the man's hand.

"I don't suppose you'd be looking for a job, Mr. Adams?" Mathis asked.

"As a matter of fact," Clint said, "I'm not."

"What brings you here, then?"

"I'm looking for a friend of mine," Clint said. "I'm supposed to have dinner with him."

"Who's your friend?"

"Charley Pearlberg."

Mathis smiled.

"I know Charley well, and I happen to know where he is at the moment," the man said. "Follow me."

Rather than follow, though, they walked side by side with Mathis directing Clint.

"You mind if I ask your full name?"

"Not at all. Clint Adams."

"I thought so," Mathis said. "What brings the Gunsmith here?"

"Like I said," Clint replied, "dinner with Charley."

"Do you know what's going on around here?"

"I know about the proposed lease on the Cherokee Strip, if that's what you mean."

"It is."

"Seems to be some people who aren't happy about it."

"Ignorant people mostly," Mathis said. "We've got representatives of over a hundred different spread here trying to make this work. We've got three hundred thousand head among us and we need that strip."

"How close is the lease to being done?"

"Close," Mathis said. "Still some dollar signs, but I think we've just about got it done. Charley's in here. I'll let you go in."

Mathis extended his hand again.

"I don't know what your business is with Charley, or if it even is business," the cattleman said as they shook hands, "but I'd like an opportunity to speak with you again before you leave, if that's all right?"

"I won't be running out," Clint said. "I'll be in town for a few days, at least."

"Excellent!" Mathis said. "We'll talk again, then."

"I'll look forward to it."

Clint turned and entered the restaurant. He spotted Charley right away and walked to his table.

"Goddamnit, Clint," Pearlberg said, jumping to his feet, "it's good to see ya."

Charley Pearlberg hadn't changed much since Clint had last seen him two or three years ago. In his fifties, he didn't look much older than he had the last time Clint had seen him, still tall and slender with the biggest hands Clint had ever seen on a man. Good hands for a cattleman.

"Good to see you, too, Charlery," Clint said.

"Come on, sit," Pearlberg said. He waved to the waiter across the room, who nodded. "I already arranged for steaks. They'll be here right away."

"Good," Clint said. "I'm starved."

"Was that Ed Mathis you were with?"

"Yes, it was," Clint said. "He showed me where you were."

"He talk to you?"

"He did. Offered me a job."

"Doin' what?"

"I didn't ask."

"You said no?"

"I said I wasn't looking for a job," Clint replied, "I was looking for you."

"How'd he take it?"

"Okay," Clint said, "although he does want to talk to me again before I leave town."

"Run into any trouble getting into the building?"

"A little," Clint said. "I left a fella lying in the street with a headache."

"Doesn't sound too bad," Pearlberg said. "At least you didn't have to kill anyone."

"Always glad of that," Clint said.

"Here are the steaks," Pearlberg said as the waiter approached with two steaming plates. "What's say we put aside conversation until we've eaten most of these."

"I'd say that sounds fine with me," Clint said, and attacked the steak with his knife and fork.

THREE

Over pie and coffee Charley Pearlberg got to the point.

"I didn't just ask you to meet me here for old times' sake, Clint," Pearlberg said.

"I wouldn't have ridden here from Texas if you had, Charley," Clint said. "I figured there was more to it than that."

"There is," Pearlberg said. "A lot more."

Clint put down his fork and sat back in his chair to listen to his friend's pitch.

"Obviously, you know what's goin' on here."

"Obviously."

"This thing has been a bitch to put together," Pearlberg said.

"How did I guess ahead of time that you'd be involved in putting this together?"

"I've got one of the biggest spreads," Pearlberg said. "Maybe not as big as Ed Mathis, but I got a lot to say about what goes on in this new association of ours."

"And? Where do I come in?"

Pearlberg sat forward.

9

"We're going to need somebody to deliver the first payment to the Cherokee."

"That's why you've got an Indian agent, isn't it?"

Pearlberg shook his head and said, "The agent works for the government, Clint. We need somebody who works for us to go with him and make sure all the money gets delivered."

"Is this the job Mathis was going to offer me?"

"I don't know," Pearlberg said. "I'm not sure what Ed is thinking. He's not exactly on the same page as the rest of us."

"What page is he on?"

"His own," Pearlberg said, "and only he knows what's written on it."

"Okay," Clint said, "never mind about pages. Talk to me in English. How much money are we talking about?"

"We're not sure yet," Pearlberg said. "Probably half of whatever we come to agree on."

"What's your gut feeling, Charley?"

Pearlberg scratched his nose, then behind an ear as he thought it over before answering.

"I'm figurin' we're gonna have to go to a hundred thousand dollars a year—at least."

"That means you'd have to deliver fifty thousand."

"Right."

Clint whistled.

"That's a lot of money to trust somebody to deliver."

"You can bet there are people in town just waiting for that delivery to be made."

"To grab the money, you mean?"

"Sure," Pearlberg said. "There's an opportunist in every bunch, in every town."

"The town I can see," Clint said. "Are you saying there's somebody within this cattleman's association who might try to grab the money for themselves?"

"That's exactly what I'm saying."

"Like Mathis?"

Now Pearlberg sat back in his chair and shook his head.

"I can't see that," he said. "Ed is the richest man in the association."

"Any idea who, then?"

"I might have a couple of ideas, but I don't want to say."

"What about the law? Wouldn't the sheriff go along to guard the money?"

"Even the law ain't above that kind of temptation, Clint."

"What about private guards? Pinkertons?"

"Same thing," Pearlberg said. "Fifty thousand is fifty thousand. It would tempt anyone."

"So why pick me?"

"I can trust you."

"You don't think I'd be tempted?"

"No."

"No chance?"

Pearlberg didn't smile.

"No chance."

"Well . . ." Clint said, feeling embarrassed at his friend's obvious confidence, ". . . that's, uh, real nice of you, Charley, to think of me that highly—"

"I do, Clint," the other man said, "or I wouldn't have sent you that telegram."

"What about the others in your association?" Clint asked. "Wouldn't they have to approve?"

"We've already discussed it," Pearlberg said. "I brought up your name and the others approved of me getting in touch with you and making you the offer."

"Offer?"

"Well, I wouldn't ask you to do it as a favor, Clint," Pearlberg said. "We'd pay you."

"What about Mathis?" Clint asked. "Was he one of the ones who approved?"

"Well, no . . . actually, there's about ten of us who've been discussing this plan."

"And what about the others?"

"Well, once you've agreed," Pearlberg said, "that is, if you agree, then we'll present the plan to the whole association for approval."

"So the next move is mine," Clint said.

"Yep."

"Charley," Clint said, "I'll have to think it over."

"I figured that, Clint," Pearlberg said, "but we don't have a lot of time here."

"Can you give me a day?"

"That's about all I can give you," Pearlberg said, "or maybe two. I think we may be two days away from coming to an agreement with the Cherokee."

"I've got to tell you I've heard some talk about town . . ."

"I know," Pearlberg said. "A lot of people are against paying the Cherokee, but hell, the land is theirs."

"Charley . . . I'll meet you here tomorrow night for dinner again, and give you my decision."

"Don't you want to know how much we're offerin' you?"

"No," Clint said, with a smile, "just meet me here tomorrow and be ready to buy me one of these steaks again."

Pearlberg smiled for the first time since Clint's arrival and said, "Ya got a deal."

FOUR

As they left the steak house and entered the lobby of the club Clint asked, "Who else is in your inner circle of ten?"

"No one you know, I'm afraid," Pearlberg said, "but they know who you are."

"Could one of them have told Mathis why I was here?"

"I don't think so," Pearlberg said. "None of us have much use for Mathis."

"And why is that?"

"He's arrogant," the other man said, "among other things."

"Was he invited to be in this circle of ten?"

"You make us sound like some secret society."

"Aren't you?"

Pearlberg hesitated, then said, "Not exactly. Ah, there's someone I want you to meet."

"Where?"

"The woman straight across the lobby."

Clint had spotted the woman on his own. She was

15

tall, dark-haired, handsome and solidly built. The business suit she was wearing could do nothing to hide the thrust of her full breasts, or the firmness of her thighs and butt.

"I saw her."

"Margaret Colby," Pearlberg said.

"And is she in your ten?"

"Oh, yes," Pearlberg said. "If we were a secret society Maggie would be a charter member. Come on, I'll introduce you. She's one of the ones who was against hiring you."

"Is that a fact? Why?"

As they started across the lobby Pearlberg said, "I'm afraid she believes most of what she's heard and read about you."

"Ah."

"Maybe meeting you will change her mind."

"That would be nice."

"Maggie!" Pearlberg called, as they approached her.

She was standing in the company of two other men, but excused herself as Clint and Pearlberg approached.

"Hello, Charley." She gave Clint an appraising look. "I suppose I don't have to guess who this is."

"Clint Adams," Pearlberg said, "Margaret Colby. Maggie, to her friends."

"Miss Colby."

"It's Mrs.," she corrected.

"I apologize."

"No need," she said. "I'm a widow—and there's no need for your condolences, either. My husband was trampled to death several years ago, and it couldn't have happened to a more rotten man."

"Ah," Pearlberg said, looking across the lobby, "I see someone else I have to talk to. I'll leave you two to get acquainted."

As he hurried away Maggie Colby raised one eyebrow and said, "I suppose he wants us to get to know one another better."

"Subtlety is not one of Charley's qualities."

"Have you known him long?"

"About ten years," Clint said.

"Did you work for him?"

"Helped him out, is more like it," Clint said.

"I understand you do that fairly often."

"What's that?"

"Help out your friends."

"What good are friends if they don't help each other?"

"I suppose," she said. "I'm afraid I don't have many friends. One of my husband's legacies, I'm afraid. He had none, ever. I'm afraid it rubbed off."

"That can always change," Clint said.

"Perhaps," she said. "Well, if we're going to get acquainted I might as well buy you a drink. After all, I'm the club member and you're the guest."

"If that's an invitation," Clint said, "I accept."

FIVE

Maggie Colby led Clint into the bar, where he ordered a beer and she a glass of brandy. There were other club members seated at tables, all giving Clint curious looks. Clint wondered how many of them were in Charley Pearlberg's secret ten.

When they seated themselves at a table Clint took a better look at Maggie. She appeared to be forty or so, but wore it very well. He thought that she had probably been very beautiful when she was a young woman, and was the perfect example of how beauty could blossom and mature.

"What are you thinking when you look at me that way?" she asked boldly.

"I was wondering why you were against Charley wanting to hire me to deliver the money."

"The discussion was that you would go with the Indian agent to guard the money," she said. "There was never anything said about you actually delivering the money."

"My mistake," Clint admitted. "Charley did say that."

"Fine."

"But you were against it, anyway."

"Your reputation precedes you, Mr. Adams."

"Clint, please," he said, "and you can't believe everything you hear about someone—especially me."

"Is that a fact?"

"Yes."

"So you're not a notorious gunman?"

"I don't doubt that some people think of me that way," Clint said, "but I don't."

"And how do you see yourself?"

He answered without hesitating.

"As someone who gets a lot more attention than he deserves . . . or wants."

"You're telling me that you're modest?"

"I wouldn't use that word at all."

"Misjudged, then?"

"That'd be more like it."

"But are you, in fact, as good with a gun as they say?"

"That would be immodest of me to comment on."

She smiled, taking several years off her age. He could see both the beauty she had been, and the beauty she was now.

"Tell me about yourself, Mrs. Colby."

"Maggie," she said. "Call me Maggie."

"That would make us friends."

"Let's just say we're more than strangers," she said. "You're friends with Charley, and he is one of my few friends."

"I see."

"My husband was a good businessman, Clint," she said, "but a terrible man, overall. So I wasn't unhappy when he left me, and he left me quite well off."

"Big spread?"

"Big enough."

"Big as Ed Mathis's?"

"Not that big," she said. "Bigger than Charley's, but he knows what he's doing and I don't."

"Charley doesn't strike me as that much of a businessman," Clint commented.

"I'll clarify that, then," she said. "He's a better cattleman than I am a cattlewoman, but I'm a better businesswoman than he is a businessman. Does that make it clearer?"

"Perfectly."

She crossed her legs but he could see nothing, as her skirt and boots overlapped. He could, however, see the shape of her left knee beneath the cloth of the skirt.

"So are you going to do it?"

"Take the job, you mean?" She nodded. "I told Charley I'd let him know tomorrow."

"Why would you not do it?" she asked. "Is the money we're offering not enough?"

"I don't know," he said. "We didn't discuss money."

"He didn't tell you how much we'd pay you?" she asked, clearly surprised.

"Didn't tell me," Clint answered, "and I didn't ask."

"So . . . you're going to make your decision without knowing the amount?" Clearly, she didn't understand this.

He smiled. "I guess I'm not much of a businessman, Maggie. I'll decide if I want to do it, and when I'm paid I'll find out how much."

"Why do it, then?"

"Because Charley asked me."

"Ah," she said, "there's that business of helping your friends."

"Exactly."

She thought about that a moment, her leg rocking up and down so that each time it came up the skirt revealed the shape of her leg to him again.

"That's admirable, I suppose."

He didn't comment.

"Ah, here comes someone you might want to meet," she said. He turned his head to the side and saw Ed Mathis approaching them.

"We've met," he said, but before she could ask how and where Mathis was upon them.

SIX

"I see you've met the most attractive member of our association," Mathis said to Clint.

"Yes, I have."

"Maggie, do you mind if I join you, or are you and Mr. Adams having a private discussion?"

"The discussion is not very private, Ed," Maggie said, "but the reason I wouldn't want you to join us is because I loathe you."

Mathis laughed, winked at Clint and said, "She's a great kidder. I'll just get a beer from the bar and join you two for a little while."

As he went to the bar Maggie stood up and said, "I can't stand that man. Perhaps we can talk again, Clint, later? In private?"

"I'll look forward to it, Maggie."

"You can keep drinking on my account," she said.

"That's a generous offer," he said, "but I'll just finish this one."

"Suit yourself," she said. "The offer is open for as long as you're in town. See you later."

She walked away just as Mathis came back over with a beer.

"Had to leave, did she?" he asked, taking her seat.

"She definitely *had* to leave."

Mathis wriggled in the chair and winked at Clint again.

"Nothing like sitting in a chair just vacated by a beautiful woman," he said.

Clint looked down at his beer mug and wondered if he should just toss it back and leave.

"Adams, I have a proposition for you."

"Actually," Clint said, "I'm not looking for a proposition any more than I'm looking for a job."

"But you are considering working for the association, right?" Mathis asked. "Wasn't that what Charley Pearlberg wanted to talk to you about?"

"What Charley and I talked about is private."

Mathis frowned.

"Look here, have I done something to offend you?"

"Not that I know of."

"Then why won't you listen to my offer?"

"It's real simple, Mr. Mathis," Clint said. "I'm not looking for a job."

"I'm talking about a lot of money here."

"That really doesn't matter to me."

"Well," Mathis said, "I guess I can't offer you what Maggie might have offered—"

Clint stood up and Mathis fell silent.

"Now you have offended me, Mr. Mathis. Excuse me."

Clint left his beer unfinished and walked away from Mathis, who remained seated, frowning after him.

• • •

Out in the lobby Clint ran into Charley again.

"How did it go with Maggie?" he asked.

"How was it supposed to go?"

"You were supposed to win her over," Pearlberg said. "She has a lot of pull with the association."

"You didn't tell me that," Clint said. "Besides, we didn't have much time together when Ed Mathis tried to join us."

"Tried?"

"She left when he went to get a beer."

"She hates him."

"Why?"

"He was good friends with her husband," Pearlberg said, "and she hated him, too."

"So I understand," Clint said. "Why'd she marry him?"

"Between you and me?"

"Sure."

"The money."

"Is that just a guess?"

Charley smiled. "Next time you talk to her, ask her."

"I might get my face slapped."

"I don't think so. Look, can you meet a few more people?"

"Your people?"

"Definitely."

"Not going to leave me alone with any of them, are you?" Clint asked.

"Not without special instructions."

"All right, then," Clint said. "Lead the way."

• • •

While Charley Pearlberg was introducing Clint around another man joined Ed Mathis in the bar, sitting in the seat recently vacated by Clint Adams.

"Was that Adams?" the man asked.

"It was."

"Didn't seem interested in what you had to say."

Mathis scowled and said, "He wasn't."

"So what do we do now?"

Mathis thought the question over, then said, "If Adams won't work for us, there's others who will."

"Others as good as him?"

"I guess we'll have to wait and find out," Mathis said.

SEVEN

After Clint met most of Charley Pearlberg's group he came to a decision about them. They didn't seem to have any use for Ed Mathis. This could have been from envy, since Mathis was the richest man in the association, with the biggest spread, but Clint chose to believe it had something more to do with Mathis's personality.

To their credit none of the group pressured him about taking the job Pearlberg had offered him. In fact, no one mentioned it. That seemed to have been left to him and Pearlberg to hash out.

By the time he was ready to return to his hotel he had not seen Maggie Colby again. Their private talk was probably going to have to wait until the next day.

He went to his hotel and had time to remove his boots, hang his gun belt on the bedpost and take off his shirt before there was a knock on the door. He retrieved the gun, held it at his side and swung the door open.

"I don't think you'll need that," Maggie said, looking at his gun, "but maybe we'll need this." She held up a bottle of whiskey.

Clint was not a whiskey drinker, but neither did he turn beautiful women away from his door.

"Come in," he said.

She entered and closed the door behind her as he holstered his gun and turned to face her.

"I didn't bring any glasses," she said. "You won't mind drinking right from the bottle, will you?"

"Is there any other way to drink whiskey?"

"Ah," she said, "a man after my own heart."

It was then he noticed that her next sip of whiskey was not her first.

"This wasn't exactly what I had in mind when I said we'd have a private conversation," she said, sitting on the bed, "but it'll do." She took a swig from the bottle and passed it to Clint.

"I prefer beer," he said, "but . . ." He took a small swallow and passed it back. "I was going to go to sleep, so why don't you tell me what's on your mind?"

She looked at him, her eyes lingering on his bare chest and then moving down his body until they came to rest on his crotch. She continued to stare as she took another swallow of whiskey.

Finally, she moved her eyes back up to his.

"I want to know if you can be bought."

"For what?"

"For fifty thousand dollars."

"I don't mean how much," he said, "I mean, for what?"

"There are people who don't want this lease agreement to go through," she said. "Some of them are outside the association, but there are others inside."

"Then why are they members?"

"Because they want to sabotage it from the inside."

"Why?"

"Why else?" she asked. "Why do these people do anything? Because they can figure out a way to make money from it."

"And who are the people on the inside?"

She sat leaning on one hand, holding the whiskey bottle with the other. Every time she gestured, it was with the bottle.

"I don't know for sure," she said. "I know who it isn't."

"Who?"

"Charley."

"Agreed."

"And I know who it likely is."

"Who?"

"Ed Mathis."

"Is that because you really think it's him," Clint asked, "or because you don't like him."

"I don't not like him," she said. "That's too tame a word. I just purely hate him."

She passed him the bottle. He took another small swallow and handed it back.

"But the reason I think it's him is because he's got the most money," she explained.

"Why is that a reason?"

"Because the people with the most money are never satisfied," she said. "They're always trying to think of a way to make more."

"And where do you fit in?"

"I have a lot of money," she said, "but not enough that I'd want to start spreading it around in the hopes of making more. I'm satisfied to keep what I've got."

"So when you asked me if I could be bought," he said, "you weren't offering to buy me yourself?"

"No," she said. "I don't want to buy you."

She looked at his crotch again and took a big swallow of whiskey.

"Not your gun, anyway."

"Maggie—"

"Charley says you're okay," she said, "and I'd like to take his word for it. If you tell me you're okay, I'll believe you."

"How do you know?"

"Because I know men, and I know when they're lying," she said. "For instance, at this very moment, do you want me?"

"Yes."

She smiled.

"See?" she said. "You're not lying. Now, can you be bought?"

"I think you're asking me if I can be bought off," he said, "and the answer is no."

"Again," she said, "you're telling the truth."

She passed him the bottle. He was about to refuse when he saw that if he didn't she'd drop it. He grabbed the bottle just as she toppled forward onto the bed, face-down.

EIGHT

Clint awoke the next morning with a firm pair of naked breasts pressed against his back. He frowned. They felt fine, but he wondered how they had gotten there. He remembered that Maggie Colby had passed out from all the whiskey she'd drunk. He'd had no choice but to stretch her out on the bed and let her sleep it off. He was also tired, though, so he stretched out next to her, she on top of the bedsheet, and he underneath it. Now they were both under the sheet and she was pressed up against him. Her breasts were pressed to his back and now he was aware of her crotch up against his butt. He could even feel the tangle of pubic hair through his underwear.

He wondered if she was awake.

Suddenly, her hand was on him. He was naked except for his underwear, so she slid her hand up and down his side, over his chest, then down over his belly to his crotch. He was erect and had been since he woke up and found her there. She stroked his penis through his un-

31

derwear, then tugged it down so that his erection sprang free and into her hand.

"Mmm," she said, "you're awake."

"So are you."

She took hold of his dick and pulled, rolling him onto his back. From there she straddled him and pulled his underwear off, tossing them into a corner of the room.

"Yes," she said, when she saw his rigid cock, "oh yes." She licked her lips and he suddenly felt like a steak dinner. He also noticed that she was totally naked.

"Maggie . . ."

"Just give me a minute," she said. "I haven't seen a man, a naked man an pretty as you, in a while."

"Pretty?"

"Well," she said, reaching down and stroking his penis, "here, anyway. My husband had the ugliest one I'd ever seen, and since he died I haven't . . . been with a man."

"Why not?"

She slid down between his legs, and he spread them for her so that she was lying on her belly between them.

"I haven't met one I wanted to be with."

"Why me?" he asked.

She stroked his penis again and asked, "Do you really want to talk about that now?"

"Well . . . no . . ."

She moved her hand and then pressed her face against his cock. His skin felt as smooth as glass, and he was hot.

"Oh, God," she said, closing her eyes and turned her face so that his penis was touching her nose. She stuck her tongue out and tasted him, then began to lick the length of him. Her licking became more avid until she finally just opened her mouth and took him in.

"Mmmm," she moaned as she started sucking him.

"Jesus," he said, lifting his butt off the bed. "Maggie . . ."

"Slow," she said. "I want to go slow. Can you last?"

"How long?" he asked.

She smiled up at him, flicking her tongue out over the head of his penis and said, "Long."

"I'll try," he said, and knew he was in for a long, hard morning.

She may not have been with a man in a long time, but Maggie Colby was a skillful lover. She continued to suck him and stroke him, and every time he was close to climaxing she'd sense it and stop. After that she'd use her mouth to inspect the rest of his body. At one point she rolled him onto his belly so she could run her mouth and tongue over his butt. She even spread his cheeks and licked him there, which almost made him finish right then and there.

Most of the time, though, she just seemed to want to hold him in her hands and take him into her mouth.

"You're amazing," she said, at one point. "My husband used to finish after a few minutes, and I was grateful for that."

"How did you get so . . . so good at this?" he asked.

"I had lovers before him," she explained. "Some of them were good, but none of them were this good."

"Just wait," he said, "until it's my turn to touch you."

She shivered and said, "I don't know if I'm ready for that yet. But I do know I'm ready for this."

She slid up onto him, straddled him again and lifted her butt up. She reached between them to take hold of him, then slid down on him, taking him inside.

"Oh my God," she said, and started to ride him up and down.

At least in this position he was able to see her large breasts as they bobbed around, and he was able to reach out and grab them, squeezing them and thumbing the nipples until she was moaning out loud.

"Oooh, Clint," she said, her tone gutteral, "this . . . is . . . so . . . go-o-o-o-d!"

He couldn't have agreed more. He held back as long as he could while she rode him and rode him. Her skin was smooth and pale, but she had a woman's body, not a girl's. Her belly was not flat, her hips were rounded and fleshy, her thighs were full. She was heavy on him and it was wonderful. He slid his hands around to cup her ass and pulled her to him every time she came down on him, adding to the sensations she was already experiencing.

Finally, though, he could hold back no longer and he exploded inside of her with a roar that was soon drowned out by her own cries . . .

NINE

"How much do I have to pay you to get you to stay around longer?" Maggie asked Clint over breakfast in his hotel.

"Well, I was planning on staying a few days," Clint said, "maybe longer, if I decide to take the job."

"Well, don't let me influence your decision," she said. "The idea that last night was just the beginning shouldn't figure into your decision at all."

"The beginning?" he asked. "I may die trying to keep up."

"Oh no," she said, "I was too pushy last night. Tonight I expect you to be in charge—that is, if you'd like me to come to your room again tonight."

"There's no question I do," Clint said, "but will you still want to if I don't take the job?"

"One's got nothing to do with the other," she said. "In fact, if you don't take it, it may leave you more time for me."

"Hmm," he said, "but maybe I shouldn't let that influence my decision."

"Maybe not."

"Uh-oh," he said, then, looking past her.

"What?"

"Don't turn around," he said. "Charley just came in."

She turned, saw Charley and waved. He spotted them and came rushing over.

"I didn't think you'd want him to see us," Clint said.

"Why not?" she asked. "I'm not hiding anything."

Charley reached the table and she said, "Pull up a chair and have some coffee."

"Thanks," Charley said, sitting down. There was already an extra cup on the table so Clint filled it from the pot.

"Thanks," Charley said again. "Clint, I just wanted to tell you that we met last night and the committee has left it up to me to hire you to go along with the money when it's delivered."

Clint looked across the table at Maggie.

"Oh yeah," she said. "That was what I came over to tell you last night. Guess I forgot."

Charley looked at them over his cup and said, "I thought you two might end up getting together."

"Well, you were right," she said.

"Using your charms to get him to take the job, Maggie?"

"Nope," Maggie said.

"That's not what she was using her charms for, at all," Clint said.

"I don't think I want to know any more," Charley said. He hurriedly finished his coffee and stood up. Clint didn't know how he'd managed not to peel all the skin off his mouth. "I got work to do."

"What's on the agenda?" Clint asked.

"Well," his friend said, "first thing I've got to do is decide who I'm gonna get for this job if you turn me down. See you both later."

As Charley left, Clint asked Maggie, "How's the agent going to feel about this?"

"We really don't care," Maggie said. "It's our money. The government has agreed to let him deliver it, but they also agreed that we could have a man go along. So he doesn't have any choice in the matter."

"Still," Clint said, "it wouldn't hurt if I met him and talked to him."

"Sure, why not?" she asked. "I'll introduce you."

"Is he out at his station?"

"No," she said, "while we're putting this deal together he's got a room at the club. As soon as we're finished here I'll take you over there and put the two of you together."

"Maggie, can I ask you a question?"

"Sure."

"A personal one?"

She smiled.

"How much more personal can we get since last night?"

"Good point," he said.

"So what's the question."

"It's about you and Ed Mathis," Clint said. "I understand he was a friend of your husband's."

"If those two could have friends, they were each other's," she said. "I didn't have much use for either of them, in spite of the fact that I married one of them."

There was a moment of silence and then she said, "You gonna ask me why I married him?"

"Well . . ."

"I'll tell you, anyway," she said. "It was for the money. See, I can be a conniving bitch when I want to be."

"Oh, I find that hard to believe."

"Don't," she said. "It's true. Are you also asking me if there's ever been anything between me and Mathis?"

"Actually—"

"I'll answer that, too," she said. "No, although he'd like there to be. You see, if I ever met a man I disliked even more than my husband, it's Ed Mathis. Does that answer all your personal questions?"

"It does," Clint said, and then added, "and even some I didn't know I was asking."

TEN

After breakfast they walked together back to the Cattleman's Club. As with the day before there were people clustered in front, some of them seated on the steps.

"They try to keep people from going in," Maggie explained.

"I know," Clint said. "I had to deal with them yesterday. Do they stop you?"

"They tried . . . once. Now they let me pass."

"Okay, then," Clint said. "You go ahead in."

"And you?"

"I'll be behind you," Clint said. "I think they may try even harder to stop me today."

"If I go with you—"

"No," he said, "you go ahead. I'll be right behind you."

"All right."

Clint remained across the street and watched as Maggie approached the building. The men on the steps laughed and said some things for her but in the end—

after squeezing between two of them—she was able to go up the stairs and enter the club.

Clint walked across the street and as he approached saw that the men on the steps were the same ones from yesterday. Maybe they had learned something.

"Well, look here," the man seated in the middle said. He was the same man Clint had dragged down the steps, banging his head in the process and leaving him laying in the street.

"I'm just going inside," Clint said. "I don't want any trouble."

"You shoulda thought of that yesterday, friend," the man said, "before you surprised me and dragged me down the steps in front of my friends."

The man stood up and spread his feet for balance on the steps. He was wearing his gun tied down. His friends scattered real quick, not wanting to be anywhere near him, or especially behind him, when the shooting started.

"Well, you ain't gonna surprise me today, are ya, friend?" the man asked.

"You never know," Clint said.

They stared at each other for a few moments until Clint realized the man wanted him to make the first move. He wondered, if he simply stood there and waited, what would happen, but he didn't want to take the time to find out.

"This is a bad reason to die, friend," Clint said. "Just to keep me from going inside."

"That and the bump on my head are reason enough to kill you," the other man said.

"You can get over a bump," Clint said. "Hell, you can even get over being embarrassed in front of your friends. But dead, that you can't get over."

"What makes you think I'm gonna be the one who gets dead?" the man asked.

Clint smiled and said, "I don't think it, friend. I know it."

"Stop calling me 'friend.' I ain't your friend. My name is—"

"I don't want to know your name," Clint said, cutting him off. "I don't need to know that to kill you. And when you're dead I still won't need to know it. Now come on, let's stop talking about it and do it. I've got business inside."

Clint's obvious confidence was starting to eat away at the man and his own started to wane. But to back down now would only embarrass him more. So it looked as if Clint wasn't going to have any choice in the matter. He was going to have to kill a man he didn't even know, for nothing but foolish reasons—stubbornness and pride.

"Hold on there!" a man's voice called out.

The suddenness of the voice almost spooked the man on the steps into drawing his gun. It was all Clint could do to stop himself from drawing and firing.

Seconds later a man appeared between them, wearing a badge.

"I'm not having this in my town," the sheriff said. He looked at Clint. "Mister, am I right that you're Clint Adams?"

"That's right."

Now he looked at the other man.

"You hear that Del?"

The man called Del widened his eyes and he said, "Clint Adams . . . the Gunsmith?"

"That's right," the lawman said. "That's who you're

about to go up against. Still want to draw your gun?"

Del licked his lips and looked around at the men who were watching the whole thing.

"Don't look at them, Del," the sheriff said. "You go ahead with this and they're just gonna walk away from your body. You got any real good reason to die today?"

"No, sir," Del said, "I don't, Sheriff."

"You mind if Del just backs off, Adams?" the sheriff asked.

"I don't mind at all, Sheriff," Clint said. He looked at Del. "In fact, I'd prefer it. Killing him would just play hell with the rest of my day."

ELEVEN

Before he went into the Cattleman's Club the sheriff asked Clint to go with him to his office.

"Gladly."

He followed the man and they did not speak until they were inside his office.

"Coffee?" the sheriff asked. "Just made it." He hung his hat on a wall peg, and his gun belt on another.

"Thanks."

The sheriff was in his early fifties, but he was fit and solid and he was obviously in control of his office. The way he stood between Clint and the other man, Del, told Clint that the man knew how to do his job.

"Here ya go," the lawman said, handing Clint a mug of coffee that was as black as night. Clint sipped it and found it stronger than any trail coffee he'd ever had.

"Too strong?"

"No such thing."

"Ah," the lawman said, "a man after my own heart."

The sheriff got his own cup and took it behind his desk with him.

43

"How did you hear I was in town?" Clint asked.

"I didn't," the sheriff said. "I recognized you."

"You mean you just came along by accident?"

"That's right," the man said. "Looks like I saved Del's life, too."

"I don't know if he'll thank you for it."

"My name's Rushton," the sheriff said, "Jack Rushton. Have a seat, please, Mr. Adams."

"Am I under arrest?" Clint asked, sitting opposite the man.

"If you were you'd be in a cell. No, I just want to talk for a little while, find out what you're doing in town."

"That's easy," Clint said. "I'm visiting a friend."

"Who would that be?"

"Charley Pearlberg."

"Charley's a good man."

"Yes, he is."

"You came just because he asked?"

"That's right."

"I guess that makes him a good friend of yours."

"Right again."

"What's he want you to do?"

"What makes you think he wants me to do anything?"

"Oh, I think even you would need more of a reason to come to Caldwell than just being invited," Rushton said. "Besides, Charley is very involved with the Cherokee Strip Livestock Association. My guess is that your presence has something to do with that and the lease."

"I think you'll have to ask Charley about that, Sheriff," Clint said, standing up. "Since I'm not under arrest . . ."

"You're free to go."

"Thanks for the coffee."

"Anytime."

Clint started for the door, but was stopped by the sheriff's voice before he could leave.

"Adams."

"Sheriff?"

"Try not to kill anybody while you're here."

"I'll do my best."

"I hope that's better than what you were about to do this morning," Rushton said.

"So do I, Sheriff," Clint said. "So do I."

When Clint entered the Cattleman's Club Maggie came rushing over to him.

"I thought you were going to be right behind me."

"So did I."

"I didn't hear any shooting."

"There wasn't any," he said. "Your town sheriff came along and prevented it."

"So you met Sheriff Rushton?"

"I did," Clint said. "How long has he been sheriff?"

"A few months."

"Seems longer than that," Clint said. "He seems comfortable in the job."

"Maybe he is," she said. "In the job, I mean, but he's only been here a few months."

Clint nodded. It was possible what he was sensing was the man's long experience as a sheriff—or, at least, as a lawman.

"You could be right," Clint said.

"Are you ready to meet Lupton?"

"Lupton?"

"The Indian agent."

"Ready as I'll ever be," Clint said.

TWELVE

The agent's name was Bill Lupton. He was in his mid-forties, rail-thin, with skin the texture and color of old leather. He had perhaps the largest nose Clint had ever seen on a person. It seemed to weigh his entire face down so that when he looked at you it was from beneath raised eyebrows all the time.

"Bill, this is Clint Adams," Maggie introduced.

"A pleasure," Lupton said, sticking out his hand. "I've heard a lot about you."

The three of them were standing at the bar and Maggie said, "I'll leave you two boys to get acquainted. I've got to go to a meeting."

As she walked off Lupton watched, as did Clint, and then they gave each other the kind of look men give each other when they've both seen something they approve of—in this case, the way Maggie's butt filled out the back of her jeans.

"I think I can guess what that meeting's about," Lupton said. "You taken the job yet?"

"No," Clint said. "I wanted to talk to you first and see how you felt about it."

"Well," Lupton said, "I'm much obliged for the consideration, but to tell you the truth I'd be tickled to have you along."

The bartender came over and Clint ordered a beer, even though it wasn't noon yet. The early hour didn't seem to be affecting anyone else's drinking.

"Is that a fact?"

Lupton looked down at his gun and said, "I know what this thing's for but I ain't never been accused of bein' able to use it right."

"Do you expect trouble while delivering the money?" Clint asked.

"I expect a lot of trouble," Lupton said. "My guess is somebody's gonna have to die for us to get that money delivered."

"Who would that be?"

"Well," the agent said, "certainly not the Cherokee. No, I'm talkin' about white men. There's fellas in this town don't want white men's money in Indian hands for a variety of reasons."

"Such as?"

"Well, for one, just because it is white men's money," Lupton said. "Also, because it's a lot of money and there's men who think they could put it to better use than the Cherokee. A lot of men just figure the Indians will use it to buy whiskey."

"What do you figure?"

"I figure they'll have a right to use it for whatever they want," Lupton said. "I got to admit, though, that Yellow Hand—their leader—does like his whiskey."

"Any other reasons?"

"I think there's some folks inside this association that don't want it to happen."

"Why would that be?"

Lupton shrugged.

"Private reasons."

"Then why be a member of the association?"

"Guess you'd have to ask them."

"The government's in favor of this, I assume?"

"They consider it a private deal between the Cherokee and the association," he said. "I'm just along as an observer, and I agreed to deliver the money because I know Yellow Hand."

"Wouldn't Yellow Hand send some braves to escort you?" Clint asked.

"They wouldn't get within fifty feet of town before somebody started shootin' at them," Lupton said. "Nope, the escort's got to come from here."

"What about the law?"

"Also just an observer," Lupton said. "It's up to the association to get the money out there safe and sound. That's where somebody like you comes in."

"And if I say no?" Clint asked. "Will you still take the money out there?"

"I'll take it out one way or another," Lupton said. "If you don't go with me they'll hire somebody else, but to tell you the truth I'd feel a lot safer with you along."

"And why's that?"

"Because I know your rep," Lupton said, "and I ain't never heard anything about you bein' a thief."

•   •   •

When Clint left the bar Maggie was standing out in the lobby, alone.

"I thought you had a meeting."

"We did," Maggie said.

"Anything decided?"

"Yep," she said, "someone suggested we pay you whatever you ask to get you to escort the money to the Cherokee."

"And who might that have been?"

"Me!" she said, with a smile. "I got personal reasons for paying you whatever you want just to keep you around longer."

"And did anyone go along with this plan?"

"They all did," she said. "Although it was Charley who seconded it."

"Why does none of this surprise me?"

THIRTEEN

Ed Mathis had been seated in the bar watching Clint talk with Bill Lupton. After Clint left, Lupton walked over to Mathis's table and sat down.

"So?"

"I think he's gonna do it," Lupton said.

"I told you we'd have to wait and see," Mathis said.

"Well," the agent said, "it sounds to me like he's doin' it."

"But he didn't say so, right?"

"Right."

"Okay, then," Mathis said.

"What are we gonna do?"

"I've got my man Wexler out working on something right now," Mathis said. "We should have some help in town by tomorrow. I don't think anything's going to happen before then."

"Look," Lupton said, nervously, "this is the Gunsmith we're talkin' about."

"He's only one man, Lupton," Mathis said, around a

51

big cigar that he was twirling in his lips. "Don't worry about it. We'll have plenty of help."

"I just don't want to get hit by no flyin' lead," Lupton said. "That ain't what I signed on for."

"You signed on to do as you're told for a lot of money," Mathis said. "Enough for you to quit this government job you hate so much."

"Yeah, well," Lupton said, "I just want to make sure I live long enough to collect."

"Stop worrying," Mathis said. "I've got everything under control."

"I hope so."

"If I say I do, I do," Mathis said. "Now, go take a walk or something. I don't want people seeing us talking together for too long."

Lupton scowled, got up and walked back to the bar. At that moment Mathis's man, Aaron Wexler, walked in and came up to the table.

"Sit down," Mathis said. "I don't want to attract attention."

Wexler sat, but the seat was too small for him. He was a big man, well over six foot four, and built wide. He was in his thirties and starting to thicken around the middle. Mathis didn't intend to ever see what the man would look like when he was in his late forties. Mathis kept himself fit, but he knew when Wexler reached his age he'd be disgustingly fat.

"What have you got?" Mathis asked.

"I talked to a few men, Boss, and they all asked the same thing," Wexler said.

"What's that?"

"Who were they gonna be goin' up against."

"What'd you tell them?"

"That we didn't know for sure, yet."

"You tell them what we're payin'?"

"Yes, sir."

"Are they on board?"

"When I told them it wasn't somethin' they had time to think about, they said yeah."

"They know I'm payin'?"

"No, sir," Wexler said, "but they know I work for you."

"They can't prove a thing," Mathis said. "Besides, I assume you told them they wouldn't get paid if they talked."

"Yessir, I did."

"Good. Do I know any of them?"

"One."

"Who's that?"

"Bud Henry."

"Henry's good with a gun."

"Yeah, he is," Wexler said, "and if I'd told him he was goin' up against the Gunsmith he might of taken the job for free. He's real eager to get a reputation."

"Well, I don't care why he does it," Mathis said, "just that he does. All right, Aaron. Good job. You can go now."

"Yes, sir."

The big man stood up and the chair creaked its gratitude.

"Check with me later this evening," Mathis said. "I should know something by then."

"Yessir."

Wexler left and Mathis sat back to enjoy his cigar.

Sheriff Rushton walked in and sat opposite Mathis, giving him a bleak look.

"What's on your mind, Sheriff?" Mathis asked. "You look like a man who's lost his best horse."

"It looks like Adams may be in town for a while."

"You talked to him?"

"I did," Rushton said. "I had to keep him from killing Del Taylor."

"That idiot!"

"He was gonna throw down on Adams until I told him who he was," Rushton said.

"And then?"

"And then I took him to my office for a little talk," Rushston said. "Just doing my job."

"Well," Mathis said, "once this thing goes off the way we want, you won't have to do that job anymore."

Rushton made a face and said, "I've been wearing a badge for too damn long, Mathis, so I better get what's coming to me."

"Don't worry, Jack," Mathis said. "We're all going to get what's coming to us."

FOURTEEN

Charley Pearlberg joined Maggie and Clint in the lobby.

"You hear about the meeting?" he asked.

"I heard," Clint said, looking at Maggie, "but I told you before, Charley, it's not the money that's going to make me decide."

"What is it, then?" Maggie asked.

"I just have to decide if this is something I want to do," Clint said.

"You got somethin' better to do?" Pearlberg asked.

"Not at the moment."

"So you're gonna do it?"

"I'll let you know later this afternoon," Clint said.

"We can tell you what we're willing to pay you," Maggie said. "It might not hurt to know."

"I do know," Clint answered. "You already said you'd pay me whatever I want."

"Well . . ." Pearlberg said, ". . . within reason."

"Don't worry," Clint said. "If you're paying a hundred thousand for the lease I'll use that as a guide."

"Some of the other boys want to meet you," Pearlberg said.

"Once I accept the job," Clint said, "I'll meet everybody."

He turned to leave.

"Where are you goin' now?" Pearlberg asked.

"For a walk."

"Mind if I come along?" Maggie asked.

"Yes, I do," Clint said. "I need to make this decision on my own, without your influence."

"I thought she already influenced you," Pearlberg said.

"You're a dirty old man, Charley," Maggie said.

"I'll be back in a while," Clint said.

"Don't get shot while you're out there!" Pearlberg called.

Clint made his way down the front steps without any problems. Del and his friends appeared to have decided to sit somewhere else.

Clint had no intention of getting shot, but he did intend to take the job Pearlberg had offered him. He just wanted to make Charley—and Maggie—wait a while longer.

It seemed to him that the deal was a good one for the Cherokee and the cattlemen. The association had every right to deliver their money without interference. He wondered where the interference was most likely to come from, though. Outside the association, or inside? And if it was from inside, who was behind it?

Pearlberg didn't seem to think it would be Mathis because of how rich he was. To Clint's way of thinking, being that rich made Mathis the perfect suspect. Men that rich usually thought about getting richer, and a hundred thousand dollars was a lot of money. Still, there could have been more than money behind somebody's desire to see that the lease deal wasn't made.

Clint decided that he'd go ahead and take the job, and then meet everyone else in the association. Maybe he'd be able to figure something out after he met everyone.

If the trouble was going to come from somebody like Del and his friends, he wasn't that worried. If there was someone with a brain behind it, that was going to make it harder.

He decided to take a turn around town and look at some faces. If there was some hired gunnies in town he might be able to recognize one or two of them. If he did he could have a little talk with them and find out who hired them—maybe even persuade them that the money wasn't enough for what they hired on to do.

And then there was Lupton himself. With cash like a hundred thousand being tossed around in his direction and him being paid as an Indian agent by the government, the temptation might just be too much for him.

Keeping a sharp eye out for trouble he started his walk around town. By the time he made his way back to the Cattleman's Club he'd give Pearlberg and Maggie his answer.

Pearlberg and Maggie came out onto the porch as Clint started to walk away.

"What do you think?" Maggie asked.

"He'll do it," Pearlberg said.

"Why doesn't he say so?"

"He's just bein' ornery," the cattleman said. "Makin' me wait."

"Me, too."

"What do you care if he takes the job or not?" Pearlberg asked. "He'll probably stay in town a few more days, anyway."

Maggie looked at Pearlberg and said, "I want this lease deal to go through, too, Charley. Don't forget that. I may be the only woman in this association, but that don't make me any less involved."

"You're right, Maggie," Pearlberg said. "Sorry for thinkin' what I was thinkin'."

"I told you before," Maggie said, "you're a dirty old man."

"Ah, I know—"

She smiled and added, "But you ain't far from wrong, either."

FIFTEEN

Del Taylor and his friends had taken their sitting to a saloon farther down the street called the Dusty Trail.

"Adams sure made a fool out of you, Del," Ted Beller said.

"You wanna face me with a gun, Ted?" Del asked.

"Hell, no, Del," Beller said. "You're better than me with a gun. We both know that."

"Then keep your mouth shut."

"I was just funnin'—"

"Well, the back of my head still hurts, so I ain't in the mood for funnin'."

"What are ya gonna do, Del?" Vince Cole asked.

"I don't know yet, Vince," Del said. "I just know that I ain't lettin' nobody get away with makin' a fool of me like that—not even the Gunsmith."

Jack Rushton walked into the Dusty Trail and saw Del and his buddies at the bar.

"Del," he said, "I'd like to talk to you for a minute."

Del looked around at his friends, then picked up his

beer and walked to a table with the lawman.

"What's on your mind, Sheriff?" he asked.

"I saved your life today."

"I know that," Del said. "I'm grateful."

"You still ain't gonna let Adams get away with what he done, though, are you?"

"There's ways of getting back at him without facing him," Del said. "You gonna stop me?"

"Not if I don't see it," Rushton said. "I can't stop you or arrest you if I don't see it. But I also wouldn't want it to happen in town."

"Why not? What do you care if you ain't around?"

"Because there'll be lots of other folks around," Rushton said. "Witnesses. You can be arrested on the say-so of witnesses."

"So what are you sayin'?"

"I'm just saying a smart man could figure out a way to do what he wanted to do without bein' seen. That's all I'm sayin'."

"I guess you're right."

"And a smart man would take along some help."

"I got help," Del said. "I got my friends."

"There's strength in numbers, Del," Rushton said, "don't forget that."

The sheriff got up and left. Del's friends came over and sat down with him.

"What'd he want, Del?"

"I ain't sure," Del said, "but I think he just gave me permission to kill Clint Adams as long as I don't do it in town."

"Now why would the sheriff want to go and do that?" Beller asked.

"Damned if I know," Del said, "but he said a smart man could figure somethin' out, so that's what I intend to do."

Clint didn't see any familiar faces around town until he got to the Dusty Trail saloon on his way back. He looked in the window and saw the sheriff sitting at a table with the fella named Del. He watched for a moment while they talked, and then the sheriff got up and left. About three other men joined Del at the table after that, and Clint kept walking. Was the sheriff warning Del away from him again? If so, why? Or were they talking about something else?

Clint knew that being a town sheriff was mostly a thankless job, and Sheriff Rushton did seem like a man who'd been wearing a badge for a long time.

Just something to keep in mind.

When Clint got back to the Cattleman's Club, Pearlberg was sitting in a chair, leaning it back against the wall with the front two legs off the ground.

"Where's Maggie?" he asked.

"Had things to do."

Clint pulled another chair over and sat next to his friend.

"Okay," he said.

"Okay, what?"

"Okay, I'll take the job."

"Oh, I knew that."

"You did?"

"Sure," Pearlberg said, "you was just tryin' to make me sweat."

"When do I meet the others?"

"Tonight," Pearlberg said. "You and me'll get a steak like we was gonna, and then we'll have a meetin' to discuss your fee."

"I'm gonna leave that up to you, Charley."

"Me?" Pearlberg asked. "Why me?"

"Because I don't believe you'd cheat me," Clint said. "I think you'll be fair."

"Well . . . of course I'll be fair. You're my friend, for chrissake."

"There ya go," Clint said. "My fee is in your hands."

"And about fifty thousand dollars," Pearlberg said, "is gonna be in yours."

SIXTEEN

Maggie Colby joined Clint and Charley Pearlberg for dinner, which neither man minded. Clint could see that Pearlberg had great affection for Maggie, much like a brother for a sister. Maybe it was even fatherly, although there was only about fifteen years or so between them.

"Who do I have to impress tonight?" Clint asked.

"Nobody," Pearlberg said. "The job is yours, especially with both Maggie and me vouching for you."

"I told them that I had personally checked you out," Maggie said.

Clint didn't look at her because he knew she'd be smirking.

"Charley, what do you know about Lupton?"

"The agent? Not much. He doesn't like his job much, I can tell you that."

"Why not?"

"Hates Indians."

"Then why does he have the job?"

"I think he pissed somebody off."

63

"And you people are going to give him fifty thousand dollars to deliver?"

"Not without you along," Pearlberg said.

"What if I had said no?" Clint asked.

"You wouldn't."

"You were sure of that?"

"Mostly."

Clint looked at Maggie.

"I hate being predictable."

"You think Lupton will try to steal the money?" Maggie asked Pearlberg.

"Maggie, I think anybody can be tempted—except Clint, here."

She looked at Clint with interest.

"Fifty thousand dollars wouldn't tempt you?"

"Not as much as some other things."

It was his turn to smirk, and it made her blush.

"What about Rushton?" Clint asked.

"The sheriff?" Pearlberg asked. "Why do you want to know about him?"

"Just curious."

"Came here a few months ago, got the job," Pearlberg said.

"Didn't run for office?"

"Nope."

"Was he hired to come here," Clint asked, "or did he come here and then get hired?"

Pearlberg frowned over his steak.

"I don't have much to do with town politics, Clint," Pearlberg said. "I guess you'd have to ask somebody on the town council."

"Is there anybody who sits on the council and is a member of the association?" Clint asked.

"Just one man," Pearlberg said.

"Who's that?"

"Ed Mathis," Maggie said.

That didn't come as any surprise at all.

"So you think Mathis sent for Rushton?" Maggie asked.

"I don't know," Clint said. "Do they seem to be old friends, or acquaintances?"

"Can't say I ever watched them that close," Pearlberg said.

"Rushton kept me from killing a man named Del earlier today," Clint said. "Either of you know him?"

"Not me," Maggie said.

"Del Taylor?"

"I don't know his last name." Clint described him.

"That's Del Taylor."

"What's he do?"

"He works on a spread near here."

"Whose spread?" Clint asked, although he thought he already knew the answer.

"Ed Mathis's," Pearlberg said.

They all fell silent for a few moments.

"I can't see what the profit would be for Mathis," Pearlberg said. "He's got the biggest spread and the most cattle. He should benefit more from the lease than anyone."

"Maybe," Clint said, "he wants to make his own deal with the Cherokee."

"I guess that's possible," Pearlberg said.

"Will he be in on this meeting tonight?"

"He'll be there."

"So when does it start?" Clint asked.

"As soon as we get there," Pearlberg said. "After all, you're the guest of honor."

SEVENTEEN

The meeting took place in a room on the second floor of the club's building. As Clint, Maggie and Pearlberg entered the other men in the room directed their attention to them. The room looked like it belonged in a cathouse, with plush chairs all over and not a meeting table in sight.

"Gentlemen," Charley Pearlberg said, "allow me to introduce Clint Adams."

There were eight other members of this inner circle of the association, apparently, and Clint had met several of them the day before, including Ed Mathis, who nodded his way.

Pearlberg took the time to introduce the others and Clint didn't even know if he'd have the time to get to know them all or even remember their names.

A man named Daniel King asked Pearlberg, "Has Mr. Adams accepted the job?"

"Why don't you ask him?"

King looked at Clint and said, "Sir?"

"Yes, I do accept," Clint said. "I'll ride along with

Bill Lupton and see to it that the money is delivered."

The men in the room voiced their approval, going so far as to pat one another on the back. Clint noticed that Ed Mathis did not participate. Maybe nobody in the room wanted to pat his back.

When the backslapping and congratulations died down Ed Mathis asked, "And what are we paying Mr. Adams?"

"That's up to Charley," Clint said. "Whatever he thinks is fair is fine with me."

That seemed to meet with the approval of everyone else, as well.

"Now I have a question," Clint said. "When is this delivery supposed to take place?"

"Well," Pearlberg said, "the deal hasn't exactly been struck yet."

"When do you expect it to be done?"

"Any day now," Dan King said.

"Uh, we realize that if it takes longer than that you might not be able to stay around," Pearlberg said.

"Unless we increase the fee," Mathis said. "I'm sure Mr. Adams would stay if we increased the fee . . . wouldn't you?"

"Since I'm leaving the amount of the fee to Charley," Clint said, "I think you can see that it's not really that much of a factor in what I'm doing. I'll stay around for as long as I can." He looked around at all of them. "If you're anticipating this deal being done within a few days, I don't think we're going to have a problem, gentlemen . . . and lady."

"Then it's settled," Pearlberg said. "One other thing: I don't think he should have to pay for a hotel while he's here. I suggest we give him a room here."

Before anyone could agree or disagree Clint said, "I'm kind of comfortable at the hotel, Charley."

"Well, that's fine," Pearlberg said. "We can pay your bill at the end of your stay."

"I second that motion," Dan King said, and it was carried without Ed Mathis saying a word.

"I've talked with Mr. Lupton, the Indian agent, and he doesn't have a problem with me going along."

"Why would he?" another man asked. "It sure beats taking all that money out there by himself."

Everyone laughed at that—everyone except Mathis, who didn't look too happy at the turn of events. Clint wondered now what exactly it was that Mathis wanted to hire him for in the first place, if not this?

"How about a drink to seal the deal?" King asked.

"Shall we go down to the bar?" Clint asked.

"Not necessary," King said. "We can have drinks brought up here. What will you have, sir?"

Over the next hour—and over drinks—Clint was able to speak to each of the gentlemen in turn, until there was only Ed Mathis and Pearlberg left. Maggie was standing with Clint while Mathis remained at the other end of the room.

"He doesn't mix much, does he?" Clint asked.

"Nobody here likes him," she said, "but he's still an important man in the cattle business."

"He was trying to hire me yesterday," Clint said.

"What for?"

"I turned him down without asking."

"Whoa," she said. "I bet that didn't sit too well with him."

"I guess not, since he's the only one in the room who hasn't come over to talk to me."

"That's okay," she said, "You don't need to talk to him. You can talk to me."

He looked at her and said, "What I had in mind for you was more than talking."

"That's why you preferred to stay at the hotel instead of moving in here?"

"I was looking after your reputation."

"I can look after my own reputation, thank you," she said. "Half of these men have been trying to get me into bed since my husband died, anyway. Knowing that I'm with you might keep them away from me."

"Well," he said, "why don't I just leave the knowing up to you, then?"

"Fine," she said. "I'll take care of everything."

"Are we done here?" Clint asked Pearlberg, who had sidled over to where they were standing.

"As far as I'm concerned we are," Pearlberg said. "Time for me to turn in, anyway."

The three of them left the room together, none of them saying a word to Ed Mathis.

EIGHTEEN

Downstairs in the lobby Clint said to Pearlberg, "Mathis didn't look happy."

"He never does, unless he's runnin' the show. Don't mind him, Clint. The rest of us can always outvote him."

"A man as rich as he is can always buy votes, Charley," Clint said. "I'm always leery of rich men."

"Not rich women?" Maggie asked.

He smiled at her and said, "Somehow I can always manage to get along with women. Rich or poor."

"Why doesn't that surprise me?"

"This is where I turn in," Pearlberg said. "Clint, breakfast?"

Clint looked at Maggie and said, "I don't think so."

"Fine," Pearlberg said. "Lunch. See you then."

Clint and Maggie walked over to his hotel together.

"You really think Mathis is against this lease?" she asked.

"You know him better than I do, Maggie," Clint said. "Why don't you tell me?"

"You have a fresher outlook on him than I do."

"Well," Clint said, "he's got something up his sleeve."

"How can you tell?"

"With men like him, I can always feel it."

"And you'll still take the job?" she asked, as they reached the front of the hotel.

"I'm probably taking the job because of him," Clint said. "If I can help the association and annoy him at the same time, that'll make me happy."

"I know something that'll make me happy," she said, putting her hand on his arm.

"Good God, woman," Clint said, "can't you wait until we get to the room?"

"I guess I can wait," she said, "but just barely."

"Then I guess we better hurry."

Ed Mathis left the meeting room after Clint, Pearlberg and Maggie and went down to the bar. He found Wexler waiting there for him.

As he went past the man he said, "Come and sit, and bring me a beer."

"Yes, sir."

Mathis sat down and waited impatiently for Wexler to join him.

"Sit down," he said, when the big man reached him.

"Yes, sir."

Wexler sat and pushed a fresh beer across the table to his boss.

"Adams took the job."

"What do you want me to do?"

"I want to talk to Bud Henry myself tomorrow."

"Here?"

"No, not here, stupid," Mathis said. "I don't want to be seen with him. Make it the back room of the Dusty Trail."

"When?"

"Make it noon."

"All right, Boss."

Wexler started to drink his own beer and Mathis said, "That's all, Wexler. You can go."

"Yes, sir."

Wexler picked up his beer and went back to the bar. Mathis didn't know how much longer he was going to be able to stall this lease deal. If it went through it might enable some of the other ranchers to expand their spreads and possibly get as big as he was. He couldn't have that. He had to be the biggest and richest, just as he was right now. The only way to make sure this lease deal didn't go through was to have that money stolen and make it look like the Cherokees' doing—and kill the people delivering it.

Lupton thought he was in this for a piece of the action, but he was expendable right from the beginning. And now Clint Adams fit into the same category.

Expendable.

When Clint and Maggie reached his room he said, "Just wait here a second."

"In the hall?" she said. "That's not very romantic."

"I want to check out the room."

"You think somebody's waiting in there for you?"

"It's not unusual for me to find women in my bed."

"I'll bet."

"Or someone waiting to put a bullet in my back."

"Oh," she said. "Well, okay, I'll just wait out here."

"Good idea."

NINETEEN

Clint checked the room and found it empty, then reached out into the hall and pulled Maggie inside. Once inside he started pulling her clothes off.

"I guess the room is safe?" she asked, while he was kissing her.

"That depends on what you consider safe," he murmured against her neck.

"Well," she said, "what I mean is that no one will bother us once we're naked."

"Then," he said, removing her shirt and tossing it into a corner, "I guess we're pretty safe."

"I don't think this is what the sheriff was talking about," Eric Slade said.

"He said make sure there were no witnesses," Del Taylor said. "Who's gonna see anything when they're all asleep?"

"Yeah, but," one of the other men said, "ain't the shootin' gonna wake people up?"

His name was Jason Gary, and Del gave him a hard look.

"We get in, we take care of Adams and we get out before anybody sees us."

"And what about the woman?" the third man asked.

"What about her, Mark?" Del asked. "I ain't gonna let no woman get in the way."

Mark Oats said, "So we kill her, too?"

"We kill anybody who's in that room," Del said, "but I get the Gunsmith."

The other three exchanged glances as Del Taylor continued to stare across the street at the hotel. They weren't sure about this, but Del Taylor wasn't the kind of man who took no for an answer when he asked for help—and none of them wanted to cross him.

"Well," Slade said, "okay, Del. You call it."

"Let's just give them some time to get comfy," Del said, "and then we'll make our move."

Clint and Maggie were more than comfy. They were naked and sprawled in the bed, exploring every inch of each other's body. Eventually, though, Clint managed to get on top.

"Remember," he said to her, "it's my turn."

She spread her arms and legs and said, "I'm yours."

He took advantage of her spread legs to slide down there and press his face to her pussy. He breathed in her fragrance and then reached out with his tongue to taste her. She gasped as his tongue slid along her already moist slit, and moaned when he began to lap up her juices.

"Mmm," he said, with his face against her, "you are a sweet-tasting woman, Maggie."

"Oh God," she said, "I hate to admit it at my age b-but . . . oooh . . . nobody's ever done that to me . . . before . . . ohhhh . . ."

"Then they don't know what they were missing," he said. He pursed his lips and kissed her there, which made her hips twitch, then slid his hands beneath her to cup her buttocks and lift her. With her ass off the bed he began to eat her avidly while she gasped and bucked and beat on the mattress with her fists.

"Jesus . . ." she gasped, ". . . oh God, don't stop . . . don't ever stop . . ."

Clint didn't intend to stop, at least not until she was completely satisfied . . . and exhausted . . .

Del told his men, "Eric and Mark you go in the back. Jace, you and me are goin' in the front."

"What about the desk clerk?" Oats asked.

"That's why you're goin' in the back," Del explained. "You go in first, come up behind the desk clerk and take care of him."

"Kill him?"

"Just knock him out," Del said. "There ain't no need to kill him, for chrissake."

"Okay, okay," Oats said, "I just thought you said we was killin' everybody."

"Everybody in Adams's room, I said."

"Stupid," Jason Gary said.

"Hey, who you callin'—"

"Both of you just shut up. Mark, you and Eric get goin'. We're givin' you ten minutes and then we're comin' in and that clerk better be taken care of by then."

"Okay, Del," Oats said, "okay."

As they drifted across the street and down a dark alley Jace asked, "Is ten minutes long enough?"

"It better be," Del said, " 'cause I can't wait no more. This throbbing in my head ain't gonna go away until Clint Adams is dead."

TWENTY

Maggie was squirming as if she was trying to get away from Clint's eager mouth, but that was not the case. She was simply squirming because she had no choice. It was either that or scream at the top of her lungs—and she was very close to doing that, anyway.

Clint could tell when she was ready to finish. He could feel her belly beginning to tremble and instead of licking her long and lusciously he began to flick at her quickly, faster and faster until finally she made a high keening noise and then let out a long gutteral groan as her legs shot straight out and went rigid, one over each of his shoulders . . .

"My God," she said, moments later, "I guess you're never too old to learn something new. I have never felt anything like that before in my life. I feel drained, I feel weak, I feel—"

"Not tired, I hope," Clint said, straddling her. His rigid penis poked at her now-soaking slit and the head slid right into her. "We're not done yet."

"Ooh, God . . ." she said, and then she almost gagged

as he drove the length of his cock into her. For a moment
he thought she wasn't going to breathe but then, as he
began to move in and out of her, her breathing started
again, although ragged.

He slid his hands beneath her to cup her ass again and
continued to work in and out of her. Her full breasts
were crushed beneath his chest and her nails were alter-
nately raking his back and his buttocks. Her heels began
to drum on the mattress at one point as she bit her lip,
and then bit him and then began to spasm again beneath
him as waves of pleasure overcame her again . . . and
then again . . . and still again, and this time he went with
her, exploding and ejaculating into her so hard that it
was difficult to tell the pleasure from the pain, except
that it all felt so good . . .

As Del Taylor came through the front door with Jason
Gary behind him the area behind the front desk looked
empty. Off to one side Oats and Slade stood, looking
extremely satisfied with themselves.

Del walked to the desk and looked over it. Slumped
on the floor was the desk clerk.

"Dead?" Del asked.

"No," Oats said, "just knocked out, like you wanted."

"Good."

Del grabbed the register, opened it and used his finger
to find Clint Adams's name and room number.

"Room fifteen," he said. He turned to the other men.
"We go up slow and quiet, we do it and then we get the
hell out as fast as we can. Pull your bandannas up over
your faces."

"Like a robbery," Oats said, suddenly understanding

that they wouldn't be recognized even if they were seen.

"That's right, Mark," Del said, pulling up his own bandanna, "just like a robbery."

When the four men had their faces covered they started up the stairs to the second floor with Del Taylor in the lead.

"If a door opens and somebody steps out of a room," he whispered, "do to them what you did to the clerk."

"Just knock them out," Oats said.

"Don't kill 'em," Slade said.

"Right," Del said.

"Stupid," Jason Gary said beneath his breath.

Clint sucked avidly on Maggie's nipples, holding first one breast in both his hands, and then the other.

"Oh, God," she said, "don't you get tired?"

"Not when I'm with a woman like you," he said, kissing her neck and sliding one hand down between her legs.

"Oooh, Jesus, no," she said, "I'm so sensitive down there if you touch me I'll . . . ohhhh . . ."

"You'll what?"

She closed her eyes real tight and said, "Scream."

"Go ahead and scream," he said, and stroked her.

She opened her mouth but no sounds came out. It was in that moment of silence that Clint heard something that saved both their lives. He didn't know what it was, and even later couldn't say. A footfall, a creaking floorboard, just something that told him that someone was in the hall . . . more than one someone . . .

"Maggie," he said.

"Yes?"

"Hit the floor . . ."

"What?"

". . . right now!" he said, and lunged for the gun hanging on the bedpost as the door crashed open.

TWENTY-ONE

Maggie hit the floor as the darkness of the room was illuminated first by light from the hall, and then by multiple muzzle flashes. The sound was deafening, and she tried to make herself as small a target as possible by rolling up into a ball.

As Maggie went off the bed at one side Clint rolled to the other. He heard the lead striking the mattress, the bedpost and the wall behind the bed. As he hit the floor he turned his gun on the doorway and fired. He heard at least two grunts as his shots struck home.

"Go, go!" somebody shouted, and the figures in the doorway disappeared.

Despite the fact that he was naked he rushed to the door but stopped right there in case someone was waiting out in the hall. He carefully stuck his head out for a look, but all he saw were two men lying on the floor.

He'd had the impression of four men crowding the door, so he'd hit two, and two got away.

"Maggie?" he called.

"I'm all right," she said. "I'm not hit. You?"

"Not hit."

"Is it . . . over?"

"It's over," he said. He looked down at the two men in the hall and could see they were dead. Slowly, doors opened down the hall and faces peered out. When they saw the dead men, though, they ducked right back in.

Clint turned and looked at Maggie, who was still seated on the floor.

"We better get some clothes on," he said. "I think we may be having company."

They were dressed and waiting when the sheriff finally showed up about ten minutes later. By that time some people had gotten brave and come out of their rooms. Also, the desk clerk had awakened and came rushing upstairs, holding the back of his head.

"Somebody hit me," he told Clint.

"Better tell the sheriff what you know," Clint suggested.

"All I know," the young man said, "is that someone hit me."

"Then that's what you tell him."

When the sheriff arrived he took charge immediately.

"Everybody back into your rooms," he said. "Go back to sleep people. It's all over."

He came down by Clint's room and bent over the fallen men. Clint had already checked them.

"They're dead," he said. "I think one or two got away."

"Looks like you were lucky," Rushton said.

"Maybe."

"I'll get some men up here to dispose of the bodies."

"Recognize these men, Sheriff?"

Rushton, who'd been in the act of turning and leaving, turned back and looked at Clint, then down at the men.

"Well, yeah," the lawman said, "I think I do. That's Jason Gary, and that one's Mark Oats."

"Who do they work for?"

"Well, I couldn't tell you that," Rushton said. "At one time or another they've worked for near everybody."

"They were with Del Taylor on the steps of the Cattleman's Club yesterday when you stopped the gunfight."

"Were they?" he asked. "I didn't notice. I know you were there, and Del. That's what I was worried about."

"They were with Taylor, and he works for Ed Mathis, doesn't he?" Clint asked.

"Does he? You know that for sure?"

"I do."

"Then you know more than me," the lawman said. "I don't keep track of who works for who. There's too much hirin' and firin' goin' on for me to do that."

"If he works for Mathis, my money says they do, too."

The sheriff squared around so he was facing Clint.

"Are you sayin' that you think Ed Mathis sent them up here to get you?"

"I'm saying it's a possibility."

"Didn't I hear that you took that job with the association?"

"I did."

"And Math is part of it," Rushton said. "Why would he send some men who work for him to kill another man who works for him?"

"I don't work for him," Clint said. "I'm working for the association."

"Same difference," Rushton said, waving away Clint's clarification of the situation. "My question stands. Why would he send someone to kill you?"

"I don't know," Clint said. "But I intend to find out."

"That's my job," Rushton said, "it's what I get paid to do."

"Fine," Clint said. "You do what you get paid to do, Sheriff. Meanwhile, I'm going to do it for free."

TWENTY-TWO

Clint and Maggie spent the rest of the night huddled together in bed. Clint used the pitcher and basin to set up a couple of booby traps to warn them if someone was trying to come in the window or the door.

"You think they'll come back tonight?" she asked, while he balanced the pitcher on the windowsill.

"No," he said, "I don't really think they'll try again tonight. I'm just playing it safe."

He came back to the bed and sat down with her.

"Maybe you'd feel better spending the night in your own room at the Cattleman's Club."

"No," she said, "somehow I feel safer here with you then I would there—if that's all right?"

"That's fine with me," he said, "but I think we better spend the rest of the night just sleeping."

"Much as I hate to say it," she said, "I think you're right."

They spent an uneventful rest of the night, then rose in the morning and got dressed. Clint noticed Maggie flexing her right arm.

"Problem?"

"Hmm? On, no, I bumped it last night when I rolled off the bed to the floor," she said. "I'm fine."

"Let's get some breakfast, then."

"What are you going to do today?"

"I don't know," he said. "Let's discuss that over breakfast."

"There are two things I can do," he said. "I can try to find Del Taylor, or I can go and confront Ed Mathis."

"He'll never admit anything," she said.

"Maybe not," Clint said, "but it will let him know that I know he was behind it."

"But what if he wasn't?"

"Del Taylor works for him," Clint said.

"Doesn't mean he ordered it."

"I'll just operate on the assumption that he did," Clint said. "It's what I think, anyway, taking into account what I've been told about him and what I've observed."

"What should I do, then?"

"Nothing," Clint said, "or whatever it is you'd be doing if I wasn't here."

"Probably sitting in the Cattleman's Club having boring conversations about cows."

They ate their breakfasts while Clint mulled things over for a bit.

"Okay, how about this," he said. "I'll try to find Del while you sit in the Cattleman's and watch Mathis. If he's behind this he's going to have to meet with somebody at some point. When he does, you'll see who it is."

"Probably Wexler."

"His foreman?"

"Aaron Wexler's not smart enough to be his foreman," she said. "He's just . . . his errand boy."

"That's even better," Clint said. "It's Wexler who will carry messages for him, but I'm betting that since things went wrong last night Mathis is going to want to talk to somebody directly."

"Like who?"

"Like somebody who'd have a better chance of killing me."

"Like . . . a gunman?"

"Maybe."

"Well, okay, then," she said, "I'll keep my eyes open."

"Good," Clint said. "Maybe if I can't find Del I can find Wexler. What's he look like?"

"You can't miss him. He's as big as a house and ugly."

"That doesn't sound hard."

"I can also go over to the Cattleman's and see how the negotiations are going."

"You're not part of the negotiations?"

"Oh no," she said.

"Why not?"

"Well," she said, "for one thing Yellow Hand would never negotiate with a white woman. For another, only Lupton, Charley and a few of the others do the actual negotiating. Then they come back and relay the information to the rest of us so we can agree, disagree or vote."

"Okay," he said, "then let's get moving. If the lease

deal, is made before I find Del I may not have the time to look for him."

They paid their bill and then left the hotel. Outside they separated, Maggie to go to the Cattleman's and Clint to go looking for Del Taylor, or perhaps Aaron Wexler.

Clint wondered if what Maggie had suggested could be right. Could it be that Mathis was not behind the attempt on his life? Was it only Del's pride that was behind the attempt?

Maggie was right about one thing. Mathis would not admit anything very freely. That meant that the most likely way to get the information was by finding Del and putting the questions to him.

TWENTY-THREE

It didn't take Clint long to find Wexler. The big man was walking down Main Street and people were stepping out of his way. Clint followed for a moment and broke off as soon as it became apparent that he was going to the Cattleman's. If he was going there to speak with his boss then Maggie would see them together. He decided to stop in and see the sheriff about what had happened the night before.

When Maggie entered the Cattleman's Club she saw Charley Pearlberg coming toward her.

"Why are you not with Yellow Hand?" she asked.

"We're on our way," he said. "What's this about a shooting at the hotel last night?"

"Somebody tried to kill Clint."

"Who did?"

"Three men, maybe four."

"What happened?"

"Clint killed two of them."

"What happened to the others?"

"They got away."

"Do you know the dead men?"

"The sheriff said they were Jason Gary and Mark Oats."

"Oops."

"What?"

"They work for Mathis."

"That's what Clint said."

"How did he know?"

"He saw them with Del Taylor yesterday, on the steps outside, and he knew that Taylor worked for Mathis."

Pearlberg scowled.

"Does he think Mathis sent them?"

"I think that," Maggie said, "but he's trying to find Taylor to ask him."

"And what are you gonna be doing?"

"I'm just going to keep an eye on Ed Mathis for a while," she said. "See who he talks to."

Dan King and the Indian agent, Bill Lupton, came along and joined them.

"Time to go, Charley," King said. He looked at Maggie. "I think we might actually come to an agreement today."

"Great."

"I'll believe it when I see it," Lupton said.

"Get the horses," Pearlberg said. "I'll be along."

"Okay," King said, and he and Lupton left.

"What's wrong, Charley?" she asked.

"There's gonna be trouble."

"There's already been trouble," she said. "Why don't you just go and do what you have to do, and let Clint handle the rest."

"I don't want anything to interfere with that money getting delivered," he said.

She put her hand on his arm and said, "Nothing will. Clint won't let it."

"I hope not," he said. "I'll see you later."

He started away and she said, "Where's Mathis?"

"I saw him having breakfast."

"Okay, thanks."

Pearlberg left the building and passed Aaron Wexler on his way out. Maggie stood where she was until Wexler committed himself to going to the dining room. She waited until he was inside, and then followed. She'd already had breakfast, but some more coffee couldn't hurt.

Ed Mathis looked up and saw Wexler approaching him.

"Sit down," he said, when the man reached his table. It was an order, not an invitation, so he didn't offer the man breakfast or coffee. "What is it?"

"Henry is all set to meet with you at noon, like you wanted."

"Good."

"Do you want me to be there, too?"

"No," Mathis said. "That won't be necessary. I can talk to him on my own."

"What do you want me to do, then?"

"Those other men you told me about," Mathis said. "Make sure they're available."

"Okay."

"Go."

As Wexler left, Mathis saw Maggie Colby sitting at a table having coffee. She seemed to be watching him.

He hadn't seen her come in. He was finished with his
own breakfast and stood up. He thought he'd spotted
something between her and Clint Adams yesterday. He
decided to go over and talk to her and see if he was
right.

TWENTY-FOUR

Clint entered the sheriff's office and found the man in much the same spot as yesterday. He was seated behind his desk with a mug of coffee, hat and gun belt hanging on wall pegs. The only difference was the whiskey bottle on his desk. As Clint walked in the lawman poured some whiskey into his cup. Clint wasn't sure there was any coffee left in it.

"Sheriff."

"What can I do for you, Adams?" the lawman asked. "As you can see, I'm a little busy." He held up his mug to illustrate just how busy he was.

"I was just wondering if you could help me with something."

Rushton took a sip from his mug and asked, "You kill somebody else? I distinctly recall askin' you not to kill anybody the last time you were here."

"Well, I didn't really have much choice in the matter last night, did I?" Clint asked.

"I suppose not."

"I was wondering if you knew where Del Taylor was."

"You still thinkin' it was Del, last night?"

"Well, the dead men were his friends."

"Can't arrest a man for havin' friends, can you?"

"I was just wondering if you were one of his friends, too?"

Rushton stopped with his mug halfway to his mouth and looked over it at Clint.

"What are you tryin' to say?"

"Only that I saw you in a saloon with Taylor yesterday," Clint said. "I thought maybe the two of you were friends, having a drink together."

"In a saloon? Yesterday?" The lawman's eyes were bloodshot. Clint wondered if he'd started drinking this early, or if he was possibly still drinking from the night before.

"The Dusty Trail? That ring a bell with you?"

Rushton thought a moment, then brightened.

"Oh yeah, I was in the Dusty Trail while I was makin' my rounds," he said. "And come to think of it, Del was in there."

"So you did have a drink?"

"Naw, naw," Rushton said, "I just went over and told him to make sure he kept away from you while you were here."

"I see."

"We ain't friends or nothin'."

"Then I guess you can't tell me where to find him."

"How would I know that?"

"I just thought maybe, in the course of doing your job, you might have come across him."

"Well, I ain't."

"Talked to Ed Mathis lately?"

"Now why would I do that?" Rushton asked sharply.

"I don't know," Clint said, with a shrug. "Just in the course of your job?"

"Well, I ain't seen him, neither," the sheriff said. "Anythin' else I can do for you?"

"No, Sheriff," Clint said, "I guess not."

"You know where the door is."

Clint nodded and left the lawman nodding, too—into his cup.

After Clint Adams left the office, Sheriff Jack Rushton poured himself a big dollop of whiskey. If Del Taylor and his crew had been successful, part of the problem would have been gone. But Del hadn't listened to his advice—or else he'd misunderstood it. In either case Adams was looking for him, now. If he found him and Del told him . . . well, then Adams might come looking for him.

He looked down at the mug full of whiskey and put it away. If he fell into that mug—again—he'd never crawl out, this time. No, he had to stay out of the whiskey long enough to see that he collected his money. And the only way to do that was to find Del before Adams did and shut him up.

He stood up, retrieved his hat and gun belt from the wall pegs and left the office.

"Mind if I sit, Maggie?" Ed Mathis asked.

Maggie was caught off guard. She'd expected to watch Mathis, not talk to him.

"Go ahead," she said. "It doesn't matter to me."

Mathis sat across from her and took out a cigar.

"I'd rather you didn't light that."

He snipped off the end and said, "Now, Maggie, that's what this club is for, men smoking and drinking . . . we never did expect to have a woman here."

"But I am here, Ed."

He smiled and lit a match. "Then I guess you'll just have to put up with the smoking and drinking."

"I can stand the smoking and drinking, Ed," she said, "it's you I can't stand."

He lit the cigar and shook out the match.

"Maggie, your husband, Ralph, was my best friend in the world, and I know he'd want me to look out for you."

"Ralph was your best friend because no one else could stand you, Ed."

He ignored the comment and continued with his thought.

"And I know Ralph wouldn't want people to see you running around with someone as low-class as Clint Adams."

"Well, you're an expert on low-class, Ed."

Suddenly, Mathis's mood changed and he frowned.

"Goddamnit, woman, what have you got against me?"

She stood up and looked down at him.

"I'll tell you what I have against you, Ed," she said. "You're just like Ralph, and I hated his guts. The only difference between you and Ralph is that he had a woman and you don't."

"I don't need any damn woman to spend my money."

"If that's all you think a woman is good for, Ed, then I feel sorry for you."

"Oh, that ain't all they're good for, Maggie," Mathis said, looking her up and down lasciviously, "I can tell you that. I know one other thing they're good for—and it's what you're giving away to Clint Adams."

Instead of getting insulted she smiled at him.

"What I'm giving to Clint, and what he's giving to me, a man like you could never understand, Ed. Never."

She turned and walked out, leaving him there with his cigar.

TWENTY-FIVE

Maggie needed some air so she went to the front door of the club. Being that close to Ed Mathis always made her feel like throwing up. When she got outside she was surprised to find Clint Adams sitting out there in a straight-backed wood chair.

"I thought you were looking for Del Taylor or Aaron Wexler," she said, sliding over to stand next to him.

"Saw Wexler walk in here before," he said. "I figured you'd know something."

"Not much," she said. "He went into the dining room and spoke briefly with his boss, then left."

"What did Mathis do then?"

"He came over to talk to me."

"How did that go?"

"Well," she said. "I got to tell him what I think of him."

"How did he take that?"

"I don't know," she said, "I left. I needed some air."

"I didn't see Wexler leave," he said. "That must have been while I was talking to the sheriff."

"What'd the sheriff have to say?"

"Not much. He looks like he's about ready to fall into a whiskey bottle."

"Doesn't sound like we accomplished much this morning," she said. "Oh, I saw Charley. He seemed to think that the association and the Cherokee are going to come to an agreement today."

"Well, good for both of them," Clint said. "Maggie, you better move on. If Mathis comes out I aim to follow him. If he stays inside then you'll have to watch him."

"I don't mind watching him," she said, "it's talking to him that makes me sick."

She put her hand on his shoulder and squeezed, and then went back inside.

Del Taylor looked out the window of his room. It was the smallest, cheapest hotel room in town, and from the window he could see the front of the Dusty Trail saloon. He also figured that from there he could take a shot at anybody he wanted.

Oats and Gary were dead and Eric Slade had left town right after they ran out of the hotel.

"I ain't stickin' around for the Gunsmith to come after me, Del," he'd said.

"Go ahead and run then," Del replied. "Who needs you? I don't need you."

"You oughta run, too, Del," Eric said. "Run as far from here as you can."

But Del didn't run, and he wouldn't. He still had a score to settle, and now he was thinking that he might just be able to settle it from this window.

He pulled a chair over to the window and sat down with his rifle leaning against the wall.

Ed Mathis checked his watch and saw that it was almost noon. Time to go and have his meeting with Bud Henry. He only hoped that Henry was as good with a gun as he was rumored to be. Better than the men he'd heard got killed last night trying to gun Adams down in his room. He didn't know who those men were, but they had almost solved his problem for him.

He was about to get up and leave the room when Sheriff Rushton came walking in.

Rushton figured the man who might know where Del Taylor was, was the man he worked for—Ed Mathis. In order to get into the Cattleman he had to walk past Clint Adams, who was seated in a chair out front.

"Good day, Sheriff," was all Clint had said, with a nod. Rushton had grunted and entered the Cattleman.

Now he walked into the dining room and spotted Ed Mathis working on a cigar.

"We have to talk," he said, joining Mathis at his table—or at what had been Maggie Colby's table.

"About what?"

"You hear about last night?"

"Word gets around," Mathis said. "Sit down, will you?"

Rushton sat.

"It was Del Taylor and some more of your men who tried to kill Adams last night."

"Del Taylor?" Mathis said. "That idiot. He never could do anything right."

"Then you did send him after Adams?"

"Of course not," Mathis said. "Why would I send a moron after Adams?"

Rushton sat back.

"Then he did it on his own because Adams embarrassed him."

"I suppose."

"Where is he now?"

"Why would I know?"

"He works for you."

"As far as I'm concerned," Mathis said, "as of now he's fired. Tell him that when you find him."

"I was going to try and find him before Adams so I could cover for you," Rushton said, "but now . . . what's the point? When Adams finds Del he won't give you away because you didn't send him after Adams."

"Idiot," Mathis said. Rushton didn't know if Mathis meant him or Del Taylor. "Look for Wexler, he'll probably know where Del is."

"Right."

Mathis leaned forward and sniffed.

"You drinking again, Jack?" he asked. "I thought you were all through with that."

Rushton stood up abruptly.

"Don't worry about me," the lawman said. "I'll do my part."

"I hope you will, Jack," Mathis said, "because that's the only way you'll get the money to retire like you want."

"I'll be in touch, Ed," Rushton said, and left the dining room.

Mathis looked at his watch. He had ten minutes to get over to the Dusty Trail.

TWENTY-SIX

Clint was still sitting outside when the sheriff came storming out.

"Did your meeting go bad, Sheriff?" Clint asked.

Rushton looked at him and for a moment Clint thought the man was going to move on without answering. But the man seemed to square his shoulders, set his jaw and turned to face him.

"I questioned Mathis about Del Taylor and his crew," Rushton said. "He had nothing to do with sending them after you."

"And you believed him?"

"Yes."

"Then you're convinced that Del came after me on his own, and brought the others with him?"

"Yes."

"And that's the results of your investigation?" Clint asked. "You're done?"

"I'll be done when I find Del," the lawman said, "not before."

"Well, that's good to hear," Clint said. "I'll look forward to that."

"Does that mean you're going to stop looking and leave it to me?" Rushton asked.

"Oh, no," Clint said, "I'm still going to look for him. See, I figure that way we have twice the chance of finding him and the other man. By the way, any idea who the other man might have been?"

"Considering who the two dead men are," Rushton said, "it's likely the fourth man was Eric Slade."

"Well, I tell you what," Clint said. "I will leave it to you to find him. How's that?"

"Thanks very much, Adams."

"Don't mention it, Sheriff."

The sheriff turned to leave, then turned back.

"Is this how you're looking for him?"

"Well," Clint said, "you can never tell who's going to walk right by here at any time of the day . . . can you?"

Rushton stared at him for a moment, then turned and started across the street.

Clint partially believed Rushton. He thought that the sheriff had gone running to Mathis—the man who got him his job—to find out if he did, indeed, have anything to do with Del Taylor. He also believed that Mathis had convinced him that he had not. And he believed it. Mathis was too smart a man to send somebody like Del Taylor after him. When somebody working for Mathis did come after him, it would be someone the rancher could depend on.

•　•　•

Mathis exited the Cattleman's moments later and was so intent on where he was going that he didn't notice Clint sitting there. Clint remained very still and gave Mathis some time and then got up and fell in behind the cattleman.

Mathis crossed the street but Clint remained on his side and followed him that way.

The wealthy rancher was walking with a very purposeful stride, as if he knew exactly where he was going and had very little time to get there.

Mathis got to the Dusty Trail and entered, going right in the front entrance. It was unknown to Clint, but not to everyone else in town, that Mathis owned the saloon, so it wasn't unusual for him to be there.

Without a word to the bartender Mathis walked to the back wall, opened a door and went in. Waiting inside was Bud Henry, sitting with one boot up on a knee, looking very calm.

"Mr. Mathis."

"Henry," Mathis said, "thanks for meeting me."

"Wexler made it sound like there was money it in," Henry said. "That's the only reason I'm here."

There was a little-used desk in the room. Mathis walked around behind it and sat down.

Bud Henry was in his mid-thirties, and had been making his way with his gun for ten years while managing to keep a low profile. He was not a man so much interested in reputation as he was in money.

"There is money in it," Mathis said, "and probably a lot more."

"What's more than money?"

"Reputation, maybe."

"I'll sell reputation for money," Henry said. "Just tell me how much we're talking about."

Mathis named a figure and Henry's eyebrows raised.

"Who do I have to kill?" he asked. "The Gunsmith?"

Clint watched as Mathis entered the Dusty Trail, and then crossed the street quickly so he could look in the window. He saw Mathis go through a door in the back.

He entered the saloon then and went to the bar. The place was mostly empty, with only one man at the bar and one man sitting at a table.

"Help ya?" the bartender asked.

"Yeah, I thought I just saw Ed Mathis walk in here, but—"

"That ain't so unusual," the barkeep said. "Mr. Mathis owns the place."

"Is that a fact?"

"He don't come in here much," the man added, "but he does once in a while."

"And is this something everybody knows?" Clint asked. "That he owns the Dusty Trail saloon?"

"Everybody but you, I reckon."

"I guess you're right."

"Get you somethin'?"

"No," Clint said, "that's all right. I've got what I wanted."

He left the Dusty Trail and took up a position across the street. It wasn't so much he wanted to see Mathis leave as it was he wanted to see who left after he did.

TWENTY-SEVEN

"So you don't want this done in town," Bud Henry said.

"No."

"I could just take him in the street, you know—"

"No," Mathis said, again, "there's more to it than that—and there's another man."

"Who's that?"

"His name's Bill Lupton."

"I know Lupton," Henry said. "He's the Indian agent, ain't he?"

"That's right."

Henry narrowed his eyes.

"This have somethin' to do with all the hubbub about the Cherokee Strip lease?"

"Why?" Mathis asked. "Would it matter to you if it did?"

"Hell, it don't matter to me if a bunch of white men want to give a bunch of Indians a lot of money," Henry said. "What do I care?"

"Okay, Bud," Mathis said, "I'll level with you. I don't want that money delivered. I want you to stop the delivery, and take care of Adams and Lupton at the same time."

"And?"

"And I wouldn't mind if it looked like they were killed by Indians."

Henry laughed. "You're lucky I don't care about reputations and such, aren't you, Mr. Mathis?" Henry asked. "Another man wouldn't want to give credit for killing the Gunsmith to a bunch of Indians."

"Will you do it?"

"I'll do it, all right," Henry said, "but for half again what you offered me."

"I offered you a lot of money."

"I know you did," Henry said. "Your first offer was very generous, indeed—but it was just your first offer, after all. You're a businessman. You know all about first offers, right?"

"Of course I do," Mathis said.

"You see," Henry said, "I just want to haggle a little bit. Isn't that what you businessmen do? Haggle?"

"Sometimes."

"So do you feel like hagglin', Mr. Mathis?"

"Not today I don't, Bud," Mathis said. "I'll agree to your terms."

"Half again?"

Mathis nodded.

"Half again," he agreed.

"Okay," Henry said, "so now all you got to do is tell me where and when the money is being delivered."

"I got some other men to help you."

"Get rid of them."

"What?"

"I'll hire my own help."

"But . . . I hired them."

"Pay them off. I don't work with men I don't know. How long have I got?"

"A day, maybe two."

"Well then, I better get on it," Henry said, standing up.

"Do you want a down payment?"

"You're a businessman, Mr. Mathis," Henry said, "A well-known businessman, and I know your word is your bond."

"So then you'll wait until after?"

"I'll just take whatever you have on you now as a down payment," Henry said.

"I . . . have a few thousand . . ."

"That'll do."

Mathis took out his wallet and handed Bud Henry what money he had in it.

"That'll do fine for starters, Mr. Mathis," Henry said. "I'm staying at the rooming house at the north end of town. You can reach me there when you have all the pertinent information."

"All right."

"If you don't mind, I'll leave first."

"Go ahead."

"Much obliged for the work," Henry said, and walked out of the room.

After Henry left, Ed Mathis opened the bottom drawer of the little-used desk and took out a metal box. He took a key from his pocket and unlocked the box. Inside were stacks of money, five thousand to a stack. He took out one stack, then closed and locked the box and put it back. He had a box like this in the bottom drawer of a desk at every business he owned. He found it always came in handy to have money around.

He put the money into his wallet, and the wallet back in his pocket then stood up and prepared to leave, himself.

Clint was waiting for Mathis to leave so when the batwing doors opened and Bud Henry stepped out he was surprised. He knew Henry was a man who made his way with a gun, but he'd never heard that he was a gunfighter. Mostly he hired out for bodyguarding, as an extra gun when range wars were happening, bank guard, the kinds of jobs that a man needed a gun for. So why was he taking this job? Or maybe Mathis was hiring for more than just facing the Gunsmith.

Maybe he was hiring him for a whole lot more.

TWENTY-EIGHT

Mathis came out of the saloon about fifteen minutes later. This time Clint was standing right there by the doors, so that the rancher almost ran into him.

"Wha—"

"You think Bud Henry's your answer, Mathis?"

"What? Who?" Mathis stammered, caught off guard.

"Bud Henry is not your answer."

"I don't know who you're talking about," Mathis said. "Bud . . . who?"

"Come on, he just came out of the saloon, and now you're coming out," Clint said. "You expect me to believe you don't know him?"

"I'm sorry, Adams," Mathis said. "Lots of people go in and out of saloons."

"Not saloons you own."

"I own a lot of businesses," Mathis said, "and lots of people go in and out of them who I don't know."

"Okay," Clint said, "play it that way. I'm just telling you I know you've hired Bud Henry."

"Look," Mathis said, "if you have a problem with a

man named . . . Bud Henry, why don't you talk to him?"

"You know what? That's a good idea. I think I will."

With that Clint turned and left Mathis standing there with his mouth open.

He spent the next half hour looking for Bud Henry but couldn't find him. As a firm opponent of coincidence he didn't believe that Bud Henry and Ed Mathis were in that saloon and didn't speak. Mathis had gone to the place for more of a reason than owning the place. He had gone there to meet someone.

Clint stopped walking and cursed. He should have stayed across from the saloon longer, seen who else came out. But no, he'd gone inside and seen three men— and none of them had been Henry. That meant that he and Mathis met in that back room.

He turned around and walked back to the Dusty Trail saloon.

When he entered the saloon the same three men were still there.

"Come back for a beer?" the bartender asked.

"Is there a back door out of here?"

"What?"

"A back way."

"In this dump?" the man asked. "Mister, there's one way in and one way out."

"What about the office in the back?"

"It's a closet with a desk," the bartender said, "No door, no window. Sorry."

"That's okay," Clint said. "That's what I wanted to hear."

"Can I do anything else for you?"

"No," Clint said, "thanks."

He left the saloon and stopped just outside. He'd doubted himself for a moment, but now he was more than convinced that he was right. Bud Henry was working for Ed Mathis.

Now he needed to find out some things about Bud Henry and he knew of one person who would have the information.

He started in search of the town telegraph office.

Clint composed a simple telegram to Rick Hartman in Labyrinth, Texas, and had it sent. It read: NEED INFOR-MATION ON BUD HENRY.

"Will you wait for an answer?" the telegrapher asked.

Clint thought a moment, then said, "No." He told the clerk to bring the answer to his hotel, or to look for him at the Cattleman's Club and gave the man five dollars.

"Yes, sir!"

When Clint got back to the Cattleman's he asked at the front desk for Maggie Colby.

"I believe she is in the dining room, sir."

Clint checked the time and saw it was lunchtime. He wondered if Mathis was also in there.

"What about Charley Pearlberg?"

"He and Mr. King and the others have not returned yet."

"Okay, thanks."

Clint turned and walked to the dining room. Sitting down and having some food and talking with Maggie might give him an idea of what to do next.

TWENTY-NINE

"There you are," Maggie said as Clint sat opposite her, so he could see the room and the door. "I got hungry." She had a bowl of what looked like beef stew in front of her

"That's fine," he said.

A waiter came running over and Clint said, "Just bring me what she has."

"Yes, sir."

"What have you managed to find out?" she asked.

"A lot, actually."

He told her that he no longer believed that Ed Mathis had sent Del Taylor after him.

"What convinced you of that?"

"He told the sheriff he didn't."

"And you believe him?"

"I believe both of them."

"Why?"

"Let me tell you the rest."

He went on to tell her about his talk with the sheriff, and about following Mathis to the Dusty Trail.

"He owns that place."

"I found that out," he said, and told her the rest.

"So who is Bud Henry?"

"Somebody who is for hire."

"To do what?"

"I'm not sure," he said. "I'm trying to find that out now. I sent a telegram and should be getting some answers soon."

"From who?"

"A friend of mine."

"What are you looking to find out, exactly?"

"How Bud Henry works," he said. "If he works with anyone, more than one, and if so, who they might be."

"How did you recognize him?"

"I have a working knowledge of who makes their living with a gun," he said. "It's just something that's handy for me to know."

"In the interest of self-preservation?"

"That's right."

"That must be a hell of a way to live."

"It is."

The waiter came with Clint's lunch and set it down in front of him.

"Thanks." He tasted it, found it excellent.

"I also talked with Mathis."

"When?"

"Twice," he said, and described both instances.

"He was lying."

"Definitely."

"He's good at that."

"I caught him off guard," Clint said. "It took him a moment to get control of himself."

"Go to the sheriff."

"No," Clint said.

"Why not? You said he confronted Mathis."

"I think he works for Mathis."

"Then why confront him?"

"Because he was worried about his own neck."

"So this Bud Henry is working for Mathis and so is the sheriff?" she asked. "Who else?"

"Maybe Lupton."

"He works for the government."

"And you know how they pay."

"Jesus," she said. "What about me? Why wouldn't you believe that I'm working for Mathis? Or Charley?"

"I know Charley," Clint said. "And you hate Mathis. You said so yourself."

"And you believe me?"

"Yes."

"So what do we do now?"

"We wait," Clint said. "Wait for my information, wait for the lease deal to be made . . . we wait."

They had moved to the bar by the time the telegraph operator came looking for Clint.

"The clerk said you'd be in here, sir," the man said. "Here is your reply."

"Thanks." Clint reached into his pocket for money.

"That's all right, sir," the clerk said. "You paid me enough."

"Thanks again."

The man left and Clint read the telegram.

"What's it say?"

"That Henry never works alone," Clint said.

"Who does he work with?"

"My friend doesn't know," Clint said. "He just says be careful, watch my back and don't expect Bud Henry to fight fair."

"That's all?"

"It's enough," Clint said, putting the telegram into his shirt pocket. "At least now I have some idea of what I'm up against."

THIRTY

Clint decided to stay around the Cattleman's the rest of the day and see what developed. That meant mostly sitting around the bar and talking to some of the other members. At one point Ed Mathis came in, but he pointedly ignored Clint and walked to what was apparently his regular table. No one joined him.

Maggie went off to do whatever it was she had to do. Clint wondered if she was the kind of woman who liked to shop. It was funny; he thought that he knew her well enough in a short time to be certain that she was not working with Mathis from within to upset the lease deal, but he didn't know if she liked to shop.

Finally, late in the day, Charley Pearlberg and Dan King entered the bar and pounded on the bar for everyone's attention.

"Gentlemen," Pearlberg said, then looked around. "I don't see Maggie, so I guess I'm safe in saying that."

There was some laughter, and Pearlberg looked so happy that Clint thought he knew what the news was.

"Gentlemen," he said, again, "we've come to an agreement with Yellow Hand."

That brought applause from the other members. Pearlberg waited for the hand-clapping to die down.

"All that needs to be done now is for the first half of the money to be delivered," he said. "The Indian agent, Bill Lupton, will be doing that with Clint Adams along to guard the money."

Pearlberg pointed over at Clint when he said his name, and that brought another round of applause.

When it died down someone shouted, "When does the money get delivered?"

"When do we take possession?" another voice asked.

"When can I move my cattle?" a third asked.

"All those details will be explained at tomorrow morning's meeting," Pearlberg said. "I just wanted to informally let all of you know that we have a deal. And now I need a drink."

He had to work his way through some backslapping before he could get to the bar for a beer, which he carried over to where Clint was sitting. Clint noticed that Ed Mathis had not participated in the applause at all.

"Congratulations, Charley," Clint said, shaking his friend's hand.

"I'll tell you the truth, Clint," Pearlberg said, "there was times I didn't think this was gonna get done."

"And now it is, except for the money."

"Right."

"When do you want it delivered?"

"Day after tomorrow," Pearlberg said. "We've arranged a meeting place with Yellow Hand. Tomorrow we'll make arrangements to get the money."

Pearlberg took a moment to greedily drink down half his beer.

"Ahhh," he said. "I been thinking about that all day. What's been happening here while I was gone? Anybody get killed?"

"Nobody got killed," Clint said, "but a lot happened," and he went on to fill his friend in.

"Wow," Pearlberg said, when Clint finished. "So where's this Bud Henry staying?"

"I don't know," Clint said. "I wasn't able to locate him, but I haven't checked all the hotels."

"And rooming houses," Pearlberg said. "There are plenty of rooming houses."

"Great."

Pearlberg shook his head. "It looks like I was wrong about Mathis. I just can't see his motive."

"There's money in it for him somewhere, Charley," Clint said. "That's the only kind of motive a man like him understands."

"Yes, but we're delivering fifty thousand dollars, Clint," Pearlberg said. "Is that a lot of money to a man like him?"

"Charley," Clint said, "that's a lot of money to anybody."

"I guess you're right. What are you gonna do now?"

"Well, I can forget about it and wait for Henry to make his move and try to take the money from Lupton and me."

"But you're thinkin' Lupton is in on it."

"Maybe he's not," Clint said, "or maybe he thinks he is but he's not supposed to come out of it alive, either."

"Why wait for them to hit you, then?"

"That's the other thing," Clint said. "I can go looking for Henry, but that means checking all the hotels and rooming houses you were talking about."

"Get some help."

"Like who?"

"Like me, for one," he said. "Like Maggie, for another."

"I don't want to put the two of you in danger."

"You're only in danger because of us, remember," Charley said. "Besides, how much trouble can we get into just checking hotel registers?"

"You have a point there," Clint said. "All right, then. As soon as Maggie gets back I'll see if she's willing."

"That woman is willing to do anything for you."

"We'll wait and see," Clint said.

Pearlberg shook his head and said, "I'm tellin, ya," and then went to the bar for two more beers.

THIRTY-ONE

Clint found out two things when Maggie returned. One, she had gone shopping.

"I needed some new boots," she said, defensively. "What's wrong with that?"

"Nothing."

Second, she was indeed willing to aid in the search for Bud Henry.

"Under no circumstances are you to talk to him," Clint told both Maggie and Pearlberg. "I'm just looking to find out where he's staying."

"We understand," Pearlberg said.

"You've only told us ten times," Maggie said.

"Well, why do I get the feeling you haven't heard me ten times?" Clint asked.

"I can't speak for Charley," she said, "but I stopped hearing you after the second time."

"Maggie—"

"Okay, okay," Maggie said, "no contact with him under any circumstances."

He looked at Pearlberg, who said, "Got it."

•   •   •

While Pearlberg and Maggie were checking hotels and
rooming houses, Clint decided to see if he couldn't get
the sheriff to deal himself out of this play.

He went to the lawman's office and entered, but for
a change the sheriff wasn't there. There was a pot of
coffee on the potbellied stove, which was still hot, so he
assumed that the man had just left, or would soon be
back. He decided to check back later, but as he was
about to leave, the office door opened and Rushton
walked in.

"Now what?" he asked Clint.

"I can't stay away from your coffee."

Rushton took off his gun belt and hat and said, "Well
then, pour me a cup while you're at it."

Clint took two mugs, cleaned them out with one finger
and filled them with coffee. He walked to the desk,
handed Rushton one and then sat down with the other
one.

"What's on your mind, Adams?"

"Want to sweeten these?"

"No," Rushton said, "get to the point."

"The lease deal has gone through," Clint said, "and
Lupton and I will be delivering the money soon."

"How soon?"

"I don't know yet," Clint lied.

"So why are you telling me this?"

Clint put his coffee down on the man's desk and
leaned forward, as if this would give more weight to his
words.

"I've decided that Mathis has been working from inside the association to sabotage the deal. Now that it's

been made I think he'll try to keep the money from being delivered."

"So you want me to keep an eye on him?"

"Sheriff, I want you to stay out of it."

"What?"

"Stay out of it."

"You want me not to do my job? Is that it?"

"No," Clint said, "I don't want you trying to help Mathis in any way. I don't know how much he's offered you, but I doubt he plans on paying off, anyway."

"How dare you—"

"Spare me the indignant act, Sheriff," Clint said. "You and I know what lawmen make, and unless I miss my guess you've been doing this kind of work for a long time."

Rushton glared at Clint but was apparently unable to contradict him.

"Now, I know Mathis is sending someone to try and stop me," Clint said. "There's a man named Bud Henry in town who hires out his gun. And Lupton doesn't make much more than you, so I'm guessing he's in on it, too."

"You're seein' lots of conspiracies, ain't you?"

"Yes, I am," Clint said, "but I don't think I'm imagining it—do you?"

Again, Rushton fell silent.

Clint stood up.

"Do yourself a favor, Sheriff, and find another way to retire," he said. "Trying to stop me isn't going to do it for you. When the time comes I won't be able to look and see who's doing the shooting before I start shooting back. It would pain me to put a hole in that badge."

Rushton flexed his fingers around his coffee mug. At

one point Clint thought the mug might shatter in the man's hand.

"Tell Mathis to get himself another badge," Clint said. "That's my free advice for the day, Rushton."

Clint turned and walked to the door.

"I really do like your coffee," he said, and left.

THIRTY-TWO

After Clint left the sheriff's office the man sat at his desk, his hand still clenched around his coffee mug. He'd tried in vain to find Del Taylor. The man was holed up somewhere, or he'd left town. Knowing how stupid he was, chances were he was still in town. But that no longer concerned Sheriff Jack Rushton. He didn't know how, but Clint Adams knew he was working for Ed Mathis. There was no way he was going after the Gunsmith when the man knew he was coming, All that was left for him to do was tell Mathis that he was dealing himself out, and then wait to get fired.

Suddenly, retirement was a long way off.

Clint left the sheriff's office and went back to the Cattleman's. There was no point in him checking hotels or rooming houses because he might be duplicating places that Pearlberg and Maggie had already been at. Besides, there weren't enough of them in town for the three of them to be checking.

It was better to go back and let Ed Mathis see him sitting around.

From his hotel window Del Taylor watched people go by. He'd seen Clint Adams outside the Dusty Trail, but he had also seen Ed Mathis there. Much as he wanted to plug Adams from his window, he couldn't do it just then. Another time he'd been lying on the bed and when he returned to the window he saw Adams leaving the saloon and didn't have time to get his rifle.

Twice in one day, and he hadn't been able to get off a shot either time. Well, if Adams had been at the saloon twice, maybe there'd be a third time.

He'd just sit and wait.

"What's he look like?" the woman who owned the rooming house asked Maggie.

"I don't know," Maggie said, "I just know his name—Bud Henry."

"Well, I got a stranger stayin' here," the older woman said, "but his name ain't—well, wait. His name is Henry."

"It is?"

"But that's his first name, not his last."

"What's his last?"

"I don't know," she said. "When I gave him the room he said just to call him Henry. I figured that was his first name."

But it could have been his last, Maggie thought. Her heart started beating faster.

She'd found him.

•   •   •

Pearlberg returned to the Cattleman's first. He hadn't had any success in finding Bud Henry or anyone named Henry in any of Caldwell's hotels. He went right into the Cattleman's bar and ordered himself a beer. Walking around was thirsty work, negotiating was thirsty work—hell, just living was thirsty work.

He turned to put his back to the bar and saw Ed Mathis walking toward him.

"Charley."

"Ed."

"Join me for a drink?" Mathis asked.

"I just got one."

"Then I'll join you," Mathis said, without so much as a by-your-leave.

Mathis waited until he had a beer in hand to speak again.

"Congratulations on pushing through that lease," he said, raising his glass.

"You never were in favor of it, were you, Ed?" Pearlberg asked, rather than raise his glass.

"Why do you say that, Charley?"

"You just always been less than enthusiastic about it."

"Maybe I just don't think a bunch of Indians should have that much money," Mathis said.

"Or anybody, huh?" Pearlberg asked. "Maybe you don't think nobody else should have money and success but you, huh?"

"Looks like you got your boy to deliver it, too, huh?" Mathis asked, ignoring the remark. "Getting everything your own way?"

"The association's way, Ed," Pearlberg said. "Not mine."

"Uh-uh."

"It wouldn't be a good idea to try and stop this, Ed."

"Is that a fact?" Mathis asked. "You threatening me, Charley?"

"I ain't threatenin'," Pearlberg said. "I'm just tellin' you, don't try to go against Clint—or the association— on this."

Mathis put his beer down on the bar hardly touched, and pushed away.

"We'll see who gets their way, Charley," Mathis said. "In the end, we'll see."

THIRTY-THREE

Clint was entering the bar just as Ed Mathis was leaving and the two men almost collided.

"Bud Henry," Clint said to Mathis. "Remember what I said."

Mathis scowled and brushed past Clint, who entered and joined Pearlberg at the bar.

"What was that all about?" Clint asked.

"I guess there's no doubt that you were right," Pearlberg said.

"About what?"

"About Mathis bein' against the lease deal," Pearlberg said. "About him workin' against it from the inside."

"He admitted it?"

"No," Pearlberg said, "but he looked me in the eye and said we'll see who gets what they want. That's just as good as admitting it."

"Sorry, Charley," Clint said.

"Don't be," Pearlberg said. "He ain't no great friend of mine, Clint. I'm just feelin' foolish that he had me fooled."

135

"Can you get him out of the association?" Clint asked.

"No," Pearlberg said, "I would need proof for that. They ain't gonna take my word for it."

"Well," Clint said, "maybe we can get you some proof."

Clint signaled the bartender for a beer.

"Well, I didn't find Henry for ya," Pearlberg said. "Maybe Maggie had better luck."

"I think I took the sheriff out of the game," Clint said, accepting his beer.

"How'd you do that?"

"Told him I knew he was working for Mathis."

"And he admitted it?"

"As good as," Clint said. "I think he's out of it."

"That's good, then," Pearlberg said. "You don't want to deal with the law, even if it's in somebody's pocket."

"Especially if it's in somebody's pocket."

They were working on their beers when Maggie walked in, saw them and hurried over.

"I found him," she said.

"Where?" Clint asked.

"A rooming house north of town," she said. "The woman who runs it says she has a man named Henry there, a stranger in town, but she doesn't know if it's his first name or last name."

"Probably him, then," Clint said. "You deserve a beer for this."

"Just a beer?"

"A beer right now," Clint said.

"Why do I feel like I'm in the way, right now?" Pearlberg asked nobody in particular.

"I appreciate what you both did today," Clint said,

getting another beer from the bartender and handing it to Maggie.

"This is all for the lease deal," Pearlberg said. "Not for you, Clint. You wouldn't be in any part of this if it wasn't for me. I'm grateful to you."

"Okay," Clint said, "but I've got a question."

"What's that?"

"When do I get paid?"

Pearlberg left Clint and Maggie at the bar after a while, saying he still had some details to take care of—including getting Clint paid.

After he left Maggie asked, "What are you going to do now?"

"I'm going to take the rest of the day off," he said. "In the morning I'll check out that rooming house and make sure it's Bud Henry staying there."

"So what are you gonna do now?" she asked.

"I don't know," he said. "We could have a late supper."

"How about," she asked, "an even later supper?"

He looked at her and asked, "My hotel?"

"Not unless we want to get shot at again," she said. She put her beer down on the bar. "Meet me upstairs in my room in ten minutes. Room eleven."

"Eleven," he said, "in ten minutes."

She smiled, turned and hurried out.

Nine minutes later Clint was getting ready to leave when Dan King came walking in.

"Clint? Do you have a minute?"

"Just barely."

"I just need enough time to have one beer and talk to you," King said. "A minute or two, no more."

Clint checked the clock on the wall and said, "Well . . . all right, Mr. King, a minute or two."

"Dan," King said, "call me Dan."

"Okay, Dan," Clint said, "we're wasting seconds here."

THIRTY-FOUR

King simply wanted to make sure that Clint knew what was expected of him, and also to make sure that Clint was being paid enough to make sure he stuck with the job.

"What makes you think I wouldn't stick with it?" Clint asked.

"Well . . . there might be some people who don't want this money delivered," King said.

"Mr. King—Dan—there are a lot of people who don't want this money delivered . . . and one of them is right here in your association."

"What?"

Clint stood up from the table they were sitting at.

"I think you'd better talk to Charley Pearlberg, Dan," Clint said. "He'll fill you in. Meanwhile, don't worry about me. I'm going to do everything I can to make sure that money gets delivered."

"Well," King said, "uh, all right . . . I'll talk to Charley then . . . but—"

"I really have to go, Dan," Clint said. "I have an urgent appointment."

He left Dan King sitting there, wondering what was going on. The man had been so busy negotiating that he just didn't know what was transpiring around him.

Clint reached room 11 not in ten minutes, but in twenty. The door was unlocked and he went in. He found himself in the main room of a suite, with light coming from the doorway of another room.

"Maggie?"

"I hope that's you." He heard her voice come from the other room. "I was starting to think you'd forgotten about me."

He went into the bedroom and saw her lying in bed with the sheet covering her. From the way it was molded to her he could see that she was naked. Her nipples were very visible as they poked up through the sheet.

"You've got too many clothes on," Maggie said.

"I think I can take care of that pretty quick," Clint said, undoing his gun belt.

Bud Henry came downstairs after his landlady came up and told him that there was a man waiting for him in the sitting room. He knew it could only be Wexler, bringing him a message from Mathis. He was surprised when he got down there to find Mathis himself waiting for him.

"Didn't expect to see you here yourself," Henry said.

"I don't have time to look for that idiot Wexler," Mathis said. "He's probably at some whorehouse."

"What's on your mind?"

"It's done," Mathis said, "the deal's been done."

"So the money gets delivered . . . when?"

"Day after tomorrow, noon," Mathis said. "Someplace between here and the delivery point you've got to get that money."

"And kill Adams and the Indian agent."

"Right. Have you got help?"

"I've got it. I'll just need to know where the delivery is going to be made."

"Why do you need to know that?" Mathis asked. "You're not going to go there."

"I need all the information about this delivery, Mr. Mathis," Henry said, "or else I don't do the job."

"All right, all right," Mathis said. "I'll get you the information by late tomorrow."

"There's something else I need, too."

"What's that?"

"You said there's a whorehouse here."

"A couple," Mathis said. "I know where one is, down the street—"

"I don't want to go there," Henry said, "I want you to send me a woman here."

"Do I look like a pimp to you?"

"I told you before I do the job—"

"All right, all right," Mathis said, annoyed. "I'll have Wexler send you a woman. What kind would you like?"

"Doesn't matter," Henry said, "as long as she's young, and white. No squaws, no niggers."

"We'll see what we can do," Mathis said. "I believe my man knows every whore in town."

"Good recommendation," Henry said.

"What about your landlady?"

"Her?" Henry said, making a face. "She's too old."

Mathis didn't laugh.

"I mean how will the girl get in?"

"Easy," Henry said. "Have her knock on the door and tell the old lady she's my sister."

"She'll believe that?"

"We'll see, won't we?"

THIRTY-FIVE

When Clint turned Maggie over onto her belly she asked, "What are you doing?"

"Wait and see."

"God," she said, as he slid his hands up the back of her calves, her thighs . . . "This is what I get for marrying an old man, for not getting more experience before I got married . . . Oohhh," she said as he touched her butt cheeks.

"You have a glorious ass," he said, running both hands over it.

"My sexual experience is so damn limit—wha-a-at is that?"

"My tongue."

"But you're putting it—oooh . . ."

Clint smiled, spread her cheeks wider and flicked his tongue, which made her hips twitch and her legs stiffen.

"There's nothing like new experiences, Maggie," he said, and bent to avidly continue his task . . .

• • •

Ed Mathis entered Milly's Cathouse and braced himself as four whores came at him.

"Girls, girls," Milly shouted, "leave the gentleman alone. Back into the parlor."

"But Milly—" a big-busted blonde complained.

"If he's interested I'll bring him in," Milly said.

Mathis was fascinated by the blonde's big breasts. He could plainly see them through her negligee, and then when she turned he was captivated by her generous ass.

"What can I do for you, Mr. Mathis?" Milly asked.

What Mathis had not told Bud Henry was that he knew where this whorehouse was because he owned it. Milly worked for him, and she was surprised to see him because be rarely came here. She made the weekly deposits at the bank and all he did was check the balance.

However, he had never been there otherwise and— what she didn't know—he had never been with a whore.

"I'm looking for my man Wexler."

"He's upstairs. He's a little, uh, occupied with Marie."

"Marie?"

"His favorite whore."

"Is she the only one he uses?"

"No," she said, "he likes Rachel and Gloria, too."

"Are they young?"

"Yes," Milly said, "they're all under twenty."

Milly herself was an old whore, meaning she had worked the cribs and houses for many years before retiring at forty to be a madam. That was five years ago.

"What about that blonde that was just here."

"That's Debra," Milly said. "She's, uh, a little older."

"How much older?"

"She's about thirty . . . two." Milly knew Debra was

thirty-eight, the oldest whore in her house.

Mathis suddenly realized why the blonde woman fascinated him. She reminded him of Maggie Colby.

"Mr. Mathis?"

"Hmm? Oh . . . Milly, I'd like you to send either Rachel or Gloria over to the rooming house at the north end of town. Do you know it?"

"I do," she said. "It's the only one there, run by old lady—"

"It doesn't matter who runs it," he said. "Have one of the girls go there, ask for Bud Henry and say that she is his sister."

"His sister?"

"Yes."

"Is she going to believe that?" Milly asked.

"I guess we'll have to see."

"Am I, uh, charging this Mr. Henry?"

"No."

"I didn't think so."

Beyond Milly, Mathis was able to see into the parlor. He could see the big blonde, Debra, sitting on a divan with her legs crossed. Her negligee was so sheer that he could see what seemed like acres and acres of pale flesh.

"Mr. Mathis?" Milly said. "Would you like me to get Wexler?"

"No," Mathis said, "leave him be. Does he spend the night here?"

"Yes, sir," she said. "Is that all right? I mean, he is your man and everything—"

"It's fine, Milly," Mathis said. "Just tell him to come and see me at breakfast tomorrow."

"Yes, sir, I will."

"All right."

He started to leave and Debra chose that moment to stretch, the movement lifting her big breasts up. Suddenly, Mathis had an extremely painful erection.

"Mr. Mathis, would you like me to send Debra to the Cattleman's Club?"

"Hmm?"

"To your room?"

"What? No, I—uh, no, that wouldn't be—"

"There's a back way into the building."

"There is?"

"Yes," Milly said, "some of the girls have used it before when—"

"When what?"

"When some of the men want to, uh, get away from their wives for a little while."

"Some of the others in the club use the girls?"

"Oh, yes, sir."

Mathis hesitated, unsure about what to do. It had been a while since he'd been with a pretty woman. His own wife was a dried-out husk he never touched anymore. Using a whore had never seemed right to him, but he couldn't keep his eyes off of Debra as she sat on that sofa.

"It's all right, sir," Milly said. "Nobody will know."

Mathis looked at her. She'd worked for him for over a year and her service had been exemplary. She was good at what she did.

"Well . . . all right," he said. "Give me a half an hour and then . . . send Debra."

"She'll be there, sir," Milly said. "She'll knock on your door in half an hour."

"All right."

"I don't think you'll be disappointed."

He needed something to take his mind off of everything. This would be ideal, he thought.

"All right," he said, again. "Thank you, Milly."

"Don't mention it, sir."

Mathis took one last look at Debra and then turned and left.

A few minutes later Milly had Rachel and Debra in her office.

"Rachel, the rooming house at the north end of town. Do you know it?"

"Yes, ma'am," the little brunette said. The three women Wexler used were small in stature. The hair color never mattered to him, as long as they were small. Why did it seem that the bigger the man, the smaller he liked his women?

"I've never been there before, but I know men who have stayed there," Rachel said.

"Go over there and present yourself as Mr. Bud Henry's sister."

"His sister?"

"That's just to get in," Milly said. "Once you're inside you'll be anything but sisterly."

"Yes, ma'am."

"And there'll be no charge."

"Yes, ma'am." She'd gone to men for no charge before. She didn't care because she got paid no matter what, and sometimes she got a nice tip.

"Go ahead."

"Yes, ma'am," Rachel said, and left.

Once Rachel was gone Debra asked, "And me?"

"Debra, you're going to the Cattleman's Club."

"Back door?"

"Yes."

"Whose room?"

"Room twenty-five," Milly said, "Mr. Mathis's room."

"Mr. Mathis?" Her eyes widened. "None of us have ever been there. He's very rich."

"Very rich, and he owns this place," Milly said. "I'm telling you that because we've known each other a long time. Don't tell the others."

"I won't, Milly."

"As far as I know Mr. Mathis has never used a whore," Milly said. "Make him happy and there could be a lot of money in it for you."

"Don't worry," Debra said, "I know how to make a man happy."

"And do it with some class," Milly said. "This could be dicey, Deb."

"How so?"

"If he wakes up tomorrow morning and regrets this it could be bad for you and me," Milly said. "If he's still happy, however, it could be very good for you and me. Do you understand?"

"Perfectly," Debra said. "I'll do my best."

"I know you will," Milly said. "I only hope it's enough."

THIRTY-SIX

Maggie snuggled up next to Clint and said, "Wow."

"I'll take that as a compliment."

"Believe me, it is," she said. "You're ruining me, you know."

"How am I doing that?"

"Once you leave I'll never find a man like you."

"Hey," he said, "all you've got to do is find yourself a young man and train him."

She laughed and said, "Ha! What would a young man want with an old woman like me?"

"You're not old."

"I would be to a young man."

"Then make it a thirty-year-old, not a twenty-year-old," he said. "One who has some experience, but can still be taught."

She hugged him tightly and said, "Why don't I just use you up while you're here and worry about that after you leave?"

He reached around and slapped her on the ass hard enough to make her squeal.

"Wha—" she said, rolling away from him.

"Come on, woman!" he said. "Use me up. I dare you."

"You—" she said, and jumped on him.

In another part of the building Debra knocked on the door of room 25. When it opened Ed Mathis stared at her. She had changed into a dress so that she was much more covered then when he had last seen her. The front, however, was cut low enough to give him a preview of things to come.

"Hello, Debra."

"Hello, sir."

"Come in."

She entered and he closed the door behind her. Mathis had the only suite in the building that had three rooms. Debra was very impressed by the expensive furnishings she saw.

"This is beautiful," she said.

"Thank you. Would you like a drink?"

"If you'd like me to have one," she said.

"Well—I mean, if you want one—"

"Mr. Mathis?"

"Yes?"

"May I speak frankly?"

"Why . . . yes, of course."

"I'm here for your pleasure, sir," she said. "If you want me to drink, I'll drink. All you have to do is just tell me what you want me to do, and I'll do it."

Mathis felt as if his tongue had gotten thicker.

"Anything?"

She smiled seductively and said, "Anything."

He stared at her for a few moments. His erection had

not subsided since the first moment he'd laid eyes on her, and now it was raging.

"Take off your dress," he said thickly.

"My pleasure . . ."

Maggie was sucking Clint's cock for all she was worth. It had become a contest between the two to see who could use who up, the kind of contest where both contestants were thoroughly enjoying themselves.

She slid her hand beneath his buttocks, as he had done to her several times now, and squeezed him while she sucked. She then slid one hand beneath his testicles to hold them and fondle them. She used her tongue, her teeth, her lips; she kissed and suckled and squeezed and he fought her as long as he could until he exploded with such force that he swore he lifted them both completely off the bed . . .

In room 25 Debra was now standing before Mathis, completely naked. He was completely mesmerized by her. Her breasts were large and, though firm, had begun to sag a bit beneath their own weight. The nipples were large and pink and already distended. Her hips were full, her thighs almost chunky. The hair between her legs was bushy and glowed like gold in the light from the room lamps.

There were times when Debra did not enjoy her job, but here she was about to have sex with a man who had more money than—well, almost anybody. That thought excited her, and the scent of her excitement filled the room. She knew he could smell her because she could smell herself—and that always excited her. She wondered if other women got excited by their own scent.

"What now, sir?"

"The bedroom," he said. "Quickly."

"Oh," she said, shaking her head, "not too quickly, I hope?"

"I—um—" That this rich and powerful man would stammer before her made her even more excited and wet. She made a sudden decision that classy was not the way to go with Edward Mathis.

She approached him and touched him, ran her hands down his chest until they came to his belt.

"I can make it last a very long time, Mr. Mathis," she said, "and the pleasure would be like nothing you've ever felt. Can I call you . . . Ed?"

THIRTY-SEVEN

Ed Mathis was in new territory. He had never smelled a woman who smelled the way Debra did. He had never felt breasts so firm in his hands, had never had his mouth on such sensitive nipples and he'd never had his penis buried deep inside a woman who felt so hot and wet and deep.

And he'd never had a woman on top of him, riding him as if she were riding for the Pony Express . . .

In room 11 much the same thing was happening. Maggie was on top of Clint, both her hands flat against his chest as she rode up and down on his rigid penis.

"God . . ." she moaned, ". . . you're the hardest . . . longest man . . . ah, jeez . . ."

When he exploded this time he knew he lifted them both off the bed . . .

Mathis also bellowed, as he exploded into Debra, whose insides seemed to be milking him. He'd never felt anything so wonderful or intense in his life. It made all the

sex he'd had in his life—with only his three wives—
seem insignificant . . . just like his three wives.

"How was it?" Debra asked.

"Amazing," Mathis said.

Debra snuggled closer to him, making sure that one
of her breasts was mashed against him.

"I'm still tingling," she said.

"Really?"

"Oh, yeah," she said.

"So it was good for you, too?"

"I saw stars," she lied. It had been okay, but she didn't
see stars.

She saw dollar signs.

"You win," Clint said.

"What?"

"I've had it," he said. "I'm done."

She reached down between his legs and took hold of
his penis. Immediately, it started to rise to the occasion.

"You liar."

"Okay," he said, "I'm not done, but I am tired. Can
we go have a late supper and then come back?"

"Well, okay," she said, "I guess I could use some
food, too."

"Is the dining room open?" he asked.

"It stays open for anyone who wants to eat at any
time," she said. "One cook, one waiter."

"Very progressive," he said.

"It was something we all voted on."

"Maybe this'll start a new wave of the future," he

said, reaching for his pants. "Restaurants open twenty-four hours a day."

She reached for her own clothes, laughed and said, "I seriously doubt that."

THIRTY-EIGHT

Clint woke the next morning with Maggie's butt up against his. It was not a bad way to wake up. They had gone down for a late supper, then returned to the room for more energetic sex, until they both drifted off to sleep.

"So who won?" she asked sleepily.

He squinted at the sun coming through the window and said, "I think it was a tie."

"That's fine with me."

"Breakfast?" he asked.

"That's fine with me, too."

As they dressed he said, "Today's the day I'll find out where the delivery will be made."

"Probably somewhere out on the strip," she said. "Have you thought about taking some other men out there with you?"

"Sure," he said, "I've thought about it, but who would I take? I don't have time to send for someone I trust."

"I can handle a gun," she said.

"No, that's not going to happen," he said. "I'd get killed while I was worrying about you."

"What about Charley?"

"Same thing."

"So it'll be just you and Lupton?"

"I guess."

"And if he's in on it," she said, "then it's just you."

"I suppose."

She stopped short of pulling on her boots and looked up at him from her seated position on the bed.

"Why do it then?"

"Because I agreed to."

"Well, speaking for the association, I release you from your agreement."

"It's not that easy."

"Then speaking for me," she said, "I'm asking you not to go."

He smiled.

"I don't think you're speaking from your head, Maggie."

"Well then wait until I can send a message to my place," she said. "I'll have my foreman bring some men and they can go with you."

"Hey, if you can get them here in time I'm all for it— as long as you can trust them."

"I can trust Hal," she said. "He worked for my husband, but he hated him, too."

"Are you and Hal . . ."

"He wishes."

"He's in love with you?"

"Yes, that's why I can trust him."

"What's wrong with him?"

She made a face and said, "Big ears."

"You mean he eavesdrops?"

"No," she said, pulling on her boots, "I mean he's got the biggest ears I've ever seen on a man."

She stood up. "I'm going to send a telegram. I'll meet you for breakfast."

"Fine," he said. "Steak and eggs?"

"Go ahead and order," she said. "It won't take me long."

She left ahead of him. He doubted she'd be able to get her men there in time, but it was a nice gesture on her part. It showed that she cared more for him than the lease deal, which could only help her in her business.

She was a hell of a woman.

Mathis woke with Debra's head between his legs. He had never come awake that way before, not with any of his wives. In fact, none of his wives had ever done to him the things that Debra had done.

He reached down to touch her head and found himself wrapping her golden hair around his fingers as she bobbed up and down on him. As he exploded into her mouth he made a sound unlike any he'd ever heard himself make before.

Later, when he tried to give Debra money she said, "Oh, I couldn't take it."

"Why not?" he asked. "It's what you do, isn't it? You're a whore."

"Yes, I'm a whore, but . . . well, I just wouldn't feel right about it. You see, I enjoyed myself as much as you did. I only take money for sex when I don't enjoy it."

Ed Mathis considered himself in complete control when he was involved in business, but with a woman like this he was a babe in the woods.

"Then just take it as a gift, Debra," he said, pressing two hundred dollars into her hand.

"All right," she said, "but just as a gift."

He walked her to the door and she kissed him deeply.

"I'm sorry you have to go out the back."

"That's all right," she said. "I wouldn't want to embarrass you. And we wouldn't want this to get back to your wife, would we?"

"My wife," he said, shaking his head. "She's a cold woman, Debra."

She'd heard that from every married man she'd ever had sex with.

"I'm sorry," she said, "you deserve to have someone warm in your life."

And as she left his room and made her way to the back door she thought, Like me.

When she got back to Milly's she found the madam in her office, sitting at her desk.

"Well?" Milly asked.

"I left him very happy."

"Great," Milly said. "You'll see, we're gonna benefit greatly from this, Debra."

"I already have," Debra said. "Here." She handed her one of the hundred-dollar bills Mathis had given her.

"He paid you? But he's the boss."

"I didn't let him know that I knew that," Debra said. "He said it was a gift."

"Wow," Milly said, "you really must have made an impression on him."

"I did."

As Debra left Milly started to wonder just how happy Debra had left Mathis, and who was going to benefit from it.

THIRTY-NINE

Maggie joined Clint at the breakfast table before the steaks were served.

"Get your telegram sent?"

"Yes."

"Good."

"You know as well as I do they'll never get here in time," she said. "And you're still going to go."

"It's not until tomorrow," Clint said. "I have today to find Bud Henry."

"And what about the others?"

"What others?"

"Others who would like to stop you from delivering the money," she said.

"I can't worry about everyone," Clint said. "There are those who would like to try to stop the money but won't. And then there are those like Bud Henry, who will do it for money."

"And Del Taylor?"

"Oh, him," Clint said. "Even if he's still in town the

163

only thing he's likely to do is shoot me in the back from hiding—if he comes up with the nerve."

"And you don't think he will?"

"I saw him yesterday," Clint said.

"Where?"

"In the window of a hotel across from the Dusty Trail saloon," Clint said. "He had a rifle, and he didn't take the shot."

"And he won't?"

"I don't think so," Clint said. "He'll stay in that hotel until he gets tired of waiting, and then he'll go on his way."

"And you'll bet your life on this?"

"Well," Clint said, "I won't be going near the Dusty Trail anytime soon, just to be on the safe side."

At that moment their waiter came with their steak and eggs. They waited until he served them and left to continue.

"So there's only Henry?"

"He's the only one I know about who is going to try to stop me," Clint said. "If I take him out of the play before tomorrow then maybe the delivery will go smoothly."

"Won't Mathis hire someone else?"

"Not if he doesn't know I've taken his man out."

"And won't Henry have help, like your friend told you in his telegram?" she asked. "Remember? He said that Henry wouldn't play fair."

Clint smiled, cut into his steak and said, "Then neither will I."

FORTY

When Bud Henry awoke that morning Rachel was lying next to him, curled up into a ball. He got down and ran his tongue along the crease between her ass cheeks. She moaned and came awake, rubbed her butt into his face as he continued to lick. Then she turned over and mounted him, because she was already wet.

Rachel had been pleased when her "brother" opened his door last night and let her in. Henry was good looking, and it was usually the homely looking one—or the married ones—that came looking for whores at Milly's. When he undressed and she saw his long, hard cock and his pretty body she knew she was in for a good night.

And now for a good morning.

Rachel was the reason Bud Henry was still in his room when Clint positioned himself across the street from the rooming house to wait for the man to come out—which was only fair.

Maggie Colby was the reason Clint was late getting there in the first place.

• • •

Clint decided not to brace Bud Henry until he knew who the other men were who would be helping him. What was the point of stopping Henry if there were still others out there?

When the hired gun came out of the rooming house he was with a girl. Clint watched as money changed hands, and then the girl kissed him on the cheek and ran off. A grateful whore was a happy whore.

After the girl left, Henry came down the steps of the house and started toward town.

Today was the day everybody would find out what they were supposed to do. Clint was sure of it. He was to find out when and where the money was to be delivered. Bud Henry would have to find out the same thing, and so would the men who were helping him. Clint was hoping that Henry would check in with his men early and not wait for the information before meeting with them.

He followed the man at a safe distance and watched as he went into a café for breakfast. If luck was truly on his side this day he would look in the window and see Bud Henry sitting with his men.

Clint walked to the café and stole a peek through the window. He saw Bud Henry join three men at a table.

So far, the luck was his.

The three men waiting for Henry looked up as he entered.

"You're late," Lenny Painter said. "We started eatin' without you."

"I had some company last night," Henry said. "Got a late start."

"Spent the night with a whore, huh?" Curly Logan said.

"That's right," Henry said, "prettiest little whore you'd ever wanna see."

"That's fine for you," the third man, Mike Killeen, said. "I had to spend the night in a hotel room with these two."

"Well, don't worry about that." Henry took out the few thousand dollars he'd gotten from Ed Mathis and handed each of the men five hundred. Their deal was 50 percent for him and 50 percent split among the other three.

"There's your payment," he said. "Now you can each get your own rooms."

"And our own whores," Curly Logan said happily, counting the money.

"Is this payment in full?" Killeen asked.

"It's half," Henry lied. It was actually little more than 20 percent of what Mathis would be paying, but intended to keep the lion's share for himself. Five hundred a piece was more money than these three men had seen in a month of Sundays, and the prospect of five hundred more when the job was done would keep them from thinking that he might be cheating them.

"You payin' for breakfast, too?" Painter asked.

"Pay for your own damn breakfast," Henry growled.

"There's the Bud Henry we know well," Killeen said.

Or not so well, Henry thought as he waved for a waiter.

Clint did not recognize the three men with Henry, but he knew the type. He saw Henry give them money and

could not believe that a businessman like Ed Mathis
would have paid in advance, so this must have been a
down payment.

He meant to see that none of these men had the time
to spend any of it—at least, not here in Caldwell.

"So when do we find out the job?" Killeen asked.

"The where and the when comes later," Henry said.

"And the who?" Painter asked.

Henry looked at them all in turn and said, "Clint Adams."

Logan whistled soundlessly.

Painter said, "No wonder it pays so much."

"This is crazy," Killeen said.

"Give me back the money if you don't want in,
Mike," Henry said. "What's the problem?"

"The problem is you're talking about the Gunsmith."

"And another man," Henry said, "an Indian agent."

"It don't matter about him," Killeen said. "The Gunsmith is the one I'm worried about."

"Again," Henry said, "what's the problem? We're
gonna know where he's goin' and when. We just have
to get ahead of him and ambush him."

"We're not takin' him head-on?" Painter asked.

"I'm not that stupid," Bud Henry said.

"It sounds okay to me, for another five hundred," Logan said.

"Me, too," Painter said.

Henry looked at Killeen.

"Mike? In or out?"

Killeen pushed away his empty plate, scowled and
said, "I'm in."

"Good," Henry said. He pushed away his half-eaten breakfast. "I'll leave first. You fellas hang around your hotel and I'll be over there later with all the information."

"When later?" Logan asked. "I want to get me a whore."

"Go and get your whore and then get back to your hotel," Henry said. "I'll be there later this evening."

He stood up, turned and left.

"Whataya think, Mike?" Painter asked.

"It's a lot of money," Logan said.

"He's gettin' more," Killeen said. "I know him."

"So what do we do?" Painter asked. "Take off with what we got?"

"No," Killeen said, "we'll stick around and wait."

"For what?" Logan asked.

Killeen looked at both of them.

"We'll wait and see if something goes wrong."

"And if it does?" Logan asked.

"Then we take what we got and get out of here," Killeen said.

"Henry'll come lookin' for us."

"There's three of us and one of him," Killeen said. "Besides, he's cheatin' us."

"How do you know?" Painter asked.

"I can feel it," Mike Killeen said, "I can just feel it."

FORTY-ONE

Clint withdrew into a nearby doorway so Bud Henry wouldn't see him when he left. He didn't know if Henry knew him on sight or not, but didn't want to take the chance. Once Henry was gone he walked to the door of the café and entered. It was a small place and no one but the three men were there. The waiter was nowhere in sight.

He walked over to the table while the three men were still counting their money and sat down.

"What the hell—" Painter said.

"Who are you, friend?" Killeen asked.

"Gentlemen," Clint said, "my name is Clint Adams, and the first man who touches his gun is dead."

The three of them froze.

"That's good. Now, one by one and only when I say, take your gun out with your opposite hand and put it on the table." He said opposite hand because he noticed one of them was left-handed.

"We can take him," Logan said. "There's three of us."

"Shut up," Killeen said.

171

"You said the three of us could take Bud," Logan reminded him.

"This is ain't Bud Henry, Curly," Painter said. "This is the Gunsmith."

"I still say we can take him."

"I tell you what, Curly," Killeen said, "you go for your gun and me and Lenny will back your play."

"Who's in a hurry to die?" Clint asked.

There was one tense moment as Clint watched all three of them, with particular attention paid to Curly, but then it was over.

"Not me," Curly finally said.

"Good. You first . . ." he said to Curly, ". . . gun on the table . . ." and then to each man in turn. They all obeyed, and when all three guns were on the table Clint pulled them over to his side. At that point the waiter came out. He was about to ask what Clint wanted when he saw the weapons on the table. He withdrew back into the kitchen.

"Smart man," Clint said, "and you three were smart not to try anything."

"What do you want?" Killeen asked.

"I don't know any of you," Clint said, "but I know Bud Henry. I know his reputation. My bet is that what he paid you to kill me is a fraction of what he's getting."

"That's what I figured," Killeen said.

"I'm giving you boys one chance," Clint said. "Take the money you got and ride out."

"B-but," Curly said, "there's more . . ."

Clint looked at him. "Not if you're dead."

"He's got a point," Killeen said.

"I know what you each look like now," Clint said. "If I see you in town, I'll kill you."

"You got a deal," Killeen said. He looked at the other two. "Let's go."

"But—" Curly started.

"I said we'd stay here until somethin' went wrong," Killeen reminded them both. "Well, it has, and so are we."

Killeen stood up.

"What about our guns?" Logan asked.

"We got enough money to buy new guns, Curly," Killeen said.

"But not until you're out of Caldwell," Clint said.

"Don't worry, Adams," Killeen said. "We're gone. Our horses are saddled and in front of the hotel and that's where we're going."

"I'll just walk along with you to make sure."

Clint walked most of the way to their hotel with the three of them in front of him, their guns wrapped up in a tablecloth in his left hand. Before long he realized that the hotel they were staying in was the cheap one across from the Dusty Trail saloon. He wondered if Del Taylor was still in the window of his room.

Del Taylor was finished. He was tired of waiting, and he wasn't even sure he'd be able to take the shot if he got a third try. He thought the best thing he could do was leave town, the way Eric Slade had done.

He was about to move away from his window when he saw three men coming down the street with Clint Adams walking behind them. He didn't know what was going on, but here was his last chance to redeem himself.

He picked up his rifle and leaned on the windowsill.

Clint took one look up at the window and saw the barrel of Del Taylor's rifle. He walked the three men to their horses and watched them mount up.

Killeen wheeled his horse around to face Clint. All three men had rifles, but none of them touched them.

"I got a favor to ask, Adams," Killeen said.

"What is it?"

"You tell Bud Henry what happened," Killeen said. "That you got the drop on us."

"I'll tell him," Clint said.

"Much obliged," Killeen said. "We don't need him doggin' us, thinkin' we stole from him."

"No problem," Clint said.

"Adios, then," Killeen said, and the three men rode out of Caldwell without looking back.

Clint realized that he had gotten underneath Taylor's rifle and the man couldn't see him from his window now. However, once he started away from the hotel he'd be right in Taylor's sites. He had to go with his gut. He did not believe that Del Taylor had what it took to kill him from the hotel window.

Clint began to back up in the street and didn't stop until he could see the window. He stood there, ready to go for his gun if he had to.

Del Taylor looked down at the man in the street. What was wrong with Clint Adams? He was just standing there, waiting. Obviously, he knew Taylor was there, which was not part of Taylor's plan. This amounted to facing Adams in the street, and he wasn't ready to do that.

He dropped his rifle out the window, turned and left the hotel room. He wasn't going to stop until he was out of town.

Redemption wasn't worth dying for.

When Taylor's rifle struck the ground Clint walked over to it, picked it up and added it to his collection. Then he turned and walked away from the hotel.

His next stop was Bud Henry, himself.

FORTY-TWO

Once again Bud Henry was elusive. Wherever he had gone Clint couldn't find him. He went back to the rooming house and asked the landlady, but she said he wasn't there, and Clint believed her. He decided to go back to the Cattleman's because that was where it had all started, and maybe that's where it would end.

When he walked in he saw a group of men standing in the lobby, and with them was Maggie. She came running over to him and grabbed his arm.

"Are you all right?"

"Fine."

"The time and place have been set," she said.

"Good. Have you seen Ed Mathis?"

"He's brooding in the bar," she said. "He was at the meeting, but didn't participate. No one looked at him or spoke to him. I think Charley may have talked to a few people."

"And you?"

"Maybe a few."

"Neither of you can prove anything."

"With some people, we don't have to."

"Well, I'm going to talk to Mathis and get this settled."

"Did you find Henry?"

"I did, but I lost him again. I found his men, though, and ran them out of town."

"What did you do?"

"I took their guns."

"Is that what's in the tablecloth?"

"Yes," Clint said. "And this rifle. I'm going to give all this iron to Mathis."

"This I've got to see."

"Well, watch from the door," he said. "I want to talk to him alone. If you're there he won't say anything damning."

"Okay."

Clint went to the bar and entered. He spotted Mathis at his usual table. The man was staring off into space. Clint walked up to Mathis and dropped the tablecloth full of guns and the rifle onto the table with a loud thud that made Mathis jump in his seat.

"What the hell—"

"This hardware belonged to the men who were going to ride with Bud Henry tomorrow, Mathis," Clint said. He opened the tablecloth up so Mathis could see the guns. "They're gone now."

Mathis stared at Clint who, for a moment, wasn't sure the man had heard him.

"I see."

"You want to tell Henry he's on his own, or should I?"

Mathis seemed to think for a moment, then he looked at Clint and said, "No, I'll tell him."

Clint was taken aback.

"You admit you hired Henry?"

"Oh, yes."

Clint frowned.

"Why the sudden turnaround, Mathis?"

"Because," the rancher said, "I've discovered something more important than money, Adams."

"What could be more important than money to you?" Clint asked, surprised.

"Well, for one thing . . . sex."

"What?"

"Did you know I own a whorehouse?"

"No, I didn't know that," Clint said. "What's that got to do—"

"I own one, but I'd never been with a whore . . . until last night. Her name's Debra. Wonderful girl. I'm going to divorce my third wife and marry her."

"You're going to marry a whore?"

"If she'll have me."

If Clint knew whores she'd have him in a second, because of his money. Did Mathis not know that?

"Oh, I'm not a fool, Adams," Mathis said. "I know that if she marries me it will be for my money, but at least she won't be a cold bitch like my other wives."

"Probably not," Clint agreed, still confused.

"You know, warmth is very important in a woman," he said, "almost as much as sex. This girl will supply both."

For a while, Clint thought.

"So you're calling this whole thing off because of a woman?" Clint asked. "Because of sex?"

Mathis thought a moment, then said, "Yes."

"How am I supposed to believe that?" Clint asked.

"I'll prove it in several ways," Mathis said. "First, the sheriff is on my payroll."

"I know that."

"You're a smart man," Mathis said. "Watch out for Lupton. I was going to pay him, too."

"Pay him, or kill him?"

"You knew about him, too?"

"I suspected."

"Well . . . nobody's dead yet, and a man can change, Adams." Mathis stood up. "I'm going to resign from the association effective this morning, and go back to my ranch. Maybe that will convince me."

"I guess delivering the money to the Cherokee tomorrow with no interference will convince me," Clint said, but he was starting to believe Mathis.

"Then that's when you'll believe me," Mathis said. "But if you'll excuse me, I have a resignation to tender. And don't worry about Bud Henry. I'll pay him off."

Clint watched Mathis leave the bar, and must have had a look of shock on his face because Maggie came rushing up to him.

"What did he say?"

"He's resigning from the association," Clint said.

"What?"

"He says the delivery will go off without a hitch tomorrow."

"B-but . . . why? What changed his mind?"

"It's the damndest thing I ever heard," Clint said.

"Apparently, all we had to do from the very beginning was get him a whore."

"What?" She looked at him as if he'd gone crazy.

"Let's sit down here and have a drink, Maggie," Clint said, "and I'll try to explain it so that we both understand it."

Watch for

THE KILLER CON

237th novel in the exciting GUNSMITH series
from Jove

Coming in September!

LONGARM

Explore the exciting Old West with one of the men who made it wild!

__LONGARM AND THE NEVADA NYMPHS #240	0-515-12411-7/$4.99
__LONGARM AND THE COLORADO COUNTERFEITER #241	
	0-515-12437-0/$4.99
__LONGARM GIANT #18: LONGARM AND THE DANISH DAMES	
	0-515-12435-4/$5.50
__LONGARM AND THE RED-LIGHT LADIES #242	0-515-12450-8/$4.99
__LONGARM AND THE KANSAS JAILBIRD #243	0-515-12468-0/$4.99
__LONGARM AND THE DEVIL'S SISTER #244	0-515-12485-0/$4.99
__LONGARM AND THE VANISHING VIRGIN #245	0-515-12511-3/$4.99
__LONGARM AND THE CURSED CORPSE #246	0-515-12519-9/$4.99
__LONGARM AND THE LADY FROM TOMBSTONE #247	
	0-515-12533-4/$4.99
__LONGARM AND THE WRONGED WOMAN #248	0-515-12556-3/$4.99
__LONGARM AND THE SHEEP WAR #249	0-515-12572-5/$4.99
__LONGARM AND THE CHAIN GANG WOMEN #250	0-515-12614-4/$4.99
__LONGARM AND THE DIARY OF MADAME VELVET #251	
	0-515-12660-8/$4.99
__LONGARM AND THE FOUR CORNERS GANG #252	0-515-12687-X/$4.99
__LONGARM IN THE VALLEY OF SIN #253	0-515-12707-8/$4.99
__LONGARM AND THE REDHEAD'S RANSOM #254	0-515-12734-5/$4.99
__LONGARM AND THE MUSTANG MAIDEN #255	0-515-12755-8/$4.99
__LONGARM AND THE DYNAMITE DAMSEL #256	0-515-12770-1/$4.99
__LONGARM AND THE NEVADA BELLY DANCER #257	0-515-12790-6/$4.99
__LONGARM AND THE PISTOLERO PRINCESS #258	0-515-12808-2/$4.99

Prices slightly higher in Canada

Payable by Visa, MC or AMEX only ($10.00 min.), No cash, checks or COD. Shipping & handling:
US/Can. $2.75 for one book, $1.00 for each add'l book; Int'l $5.00 for one book, $1.00 for each
add'l. Call (800) 788-6262 or (201) 933-9292, fax (201) 896-8569 or mail your orders to:

Penguin Putnam Inc.   Bill my: ☐ Visa ☐ MasterCard ☐ Amex _____ (expires)
P.O. Box 12289, Dept. B
Newark, NJ 07101-5289   Card# _____
Please allow 4-6 weeks for delivery.   Signature _____
Foreign and Canadian delivery 6-8 weeks.

Bill to:

Name _____

Address _____ City _____

State/ZIP _____ Daytime Phone # _____

Ship to:

Name _____ Book Total $ _____

Address _____ Applicable Sales Tax $ _____

City _____ Postage & Handling $ _____

State/ZIP _____ Total Amount Due $ _____

This offer subject to change without notice.   Ad # 201 (8/00)

JAKE LOGAN
TODAY'S HOTTEST ACTION WESTERN!

❑ SLOCUM AND THE WOLF HUNT #237	0-515-12413-3/$4.99
❑ SLOCUM AND THE BARONESS #238	0-515-12436-2/$4.99
❑ SLOCUM AND THE COMANCHE PRINCESS #239	0-515-12449-4/$4.99
❑ SLOCUM AND THE LIVE OAK BOYS #240	0-515-12467-2/$4.99
❑ SLOCUM AND THE BIG THREE #241	0-515-12484-2/$4.99
❑ SLOCUM AT SCORPION BEND #242	0-515-12510-5/$4.99
❑ SLOCUM AND THE BUFFALO HUNTER #243	0-515-12518-0/$4.99
❑ SLOCUM AND THE YELLOW ROSE OF TEXAS #244	0-515-12532-6/$4.99
❑ SLOCUM AND THE LADY FROM ABILENE #245	0-515-12555-5/$4.99
❑ SLOCUM GIANT: SLOCUM AND THE THREE WIVES	0-515-12569-5/$5.99
❑ SLOCUM AND THE CATTLE KING #246	0-515-12571-7/$4.99
❑ SLOCUM #247: DEAD MAN'S SPURS	0-515-12613-6/$4.99
❑ SLOCUM #248: SHOWDOWN AT SHILOH	0-515-12659-4/$4.99
❑ SLOCUM AND THE KETCHEM GANG #249	0-515-12686-1/$4.99
❑ SLOCUM AND THE JERSEY LILY #250	0-515-12706-X/$4.99
❑ SLOCUM AND THE GAMBLER'S WOMAN #251	0-515-12733-7/$4.99
❑ SLOCUM AND THE GUNRUNNERS #252	0-515-12754-X/$4.99
❑ SLOCUM AND THE NEBRASKA STORM #253	0-515-12769-8/$4.99
❑ SLOCUM #254: SLOCUM'S CLOSE CALL	0-515-12789-2/$4.99
❑ SLOCUM AND THE UNDERTAKER #255	0-515-12807-4/$4.99
❑ SLOCUM AND THE POMO CHIEF #256	0-515-12838-4/$4.99

Prices slightly higher in Canada

Payable by Visa, MC or AMEX only ($10.00 min.), No cash, checks or COD. Shipping & handling:
US/Can. $2.75 for one book, $1.00 for each add'l book; Int'l $5.00 for one book, $1.00 for each
add'l. Call (800) 788-6262 or (201) 933-9292, fax (201) 896-8569 or mail your orders to:

Penguin Putnam Inc.   Bill my: ❑ Visa ❑ MasterCard ❑ Amex _____ (expires)
P.O. Box 12289, Dept. B
Newark, NJ 07101-5289   Card# _____
Please allow 4-6 weeks for delivery.   Signature _____
Foreign and Canadian delivery 6-8 weeks.

Bill to:

Name _____

Address _____ City _____

State/ZIP _____ Daytime Phone # _____

Ship to:

Name _____ Book Total $ _____

Address _____ Applicable Sales Tax $ _____

City _____ Postage & Handling $ _____

State/ZIP _____ Total Amount Due $ _____

This offer subject to change without notice.   Ad # 202 (8/00)

J. R. ROBERTS
THE GUNSMITH

__THE GUNSMITH #197:	APACHE RAID	0-515-12293-9/$4.99
__THE GUNSMITH #198:	THE LADY KILLERS	0-515-12303-X/$4.99
__THE GUNSMITH #199:	DENVER DESPERADOES	0-515-12341-2/$4.99
__THE GUNSMITH #200:	THE JAMES BOYS	0-515-12357-9/$4.99
__THE GUNSMITH #201:	THE GAMBLER	0-515-12373-0/$4.99
__THE GUNSMITH #202:	VIGILANTE JUSTICE	0-515-12393-5/$4.99
__THE GUNSMITH #203:	DEAD MAN'S BLUFF	0-515-12414-1/$4.99
__THE GUNSMITH #204:	WOMEN ON THE RUN	0-515-12438-9/$4.99
__THE GUNSMITH #205:	THE GAMBLER'S GIRL	0-515-12451-6/$4.99
__THE GUNSMITH #206:	LEGEND OF THE PIASA BIRD	
		0-515-12469-9/$4.99
__THE GUNSMITH #207:	KANSAS CITY KILLING	0-515-12486-9/$4.99
__THE GUNSMITH #208:	THE LAST BOUNTY	0-515-12512-1/$4.99
__THE GUNSMITH #209:	DEATH TIMES FIVE	0-515-12520-2/$4.99
__THE GUNSMITH #210:	MAXIMILIAN'S TREASURE	0-515-12534-2/$4.99
__THE GUNSMITH #211:	SON OF A GUNSMITH	0-515-12557-1/$4.99
__THE GUNSMITH #212:	FAMILY FEUD	0-515-12573-3/$4.99
__THE GUNSMITH #213:	STRANGLER'S VENDETTA	0-515-12615-2/$4.99
__THE GUNSMITH #214:	THE BORTON FAMILY GAME	
		0-515-12661-6/$4.99
__THE GUNSMITH #215:	SHOWDOWN AT DAYLIGHT	0-515-12688-8/$4.99
__THE GUNSMITH #216:	THE MAN FROM PECULIAR	0-515-12708-6/$4.99
__THE GUNSMITH #217:	AMBUSH AT BLACK ROCK	0-515-12735-3/$4.99
__THE GUNSMITH #218:	THE CLEVELAND CONNECTION	
		0-515-12756-6/$4.99
__THE GUNSMITH #219:	THE BROTHEL INSPECTOR	0-515-12771-X/$4.99
__THE GUNSMITH #220:	END OF THE TRAIL	0-515-12791-4/$4.99
__THE GUNSMITH #221:	DANGEROUS BREED	0-515-12809-0/$4.99

Prices slightly higher in Canada

Payable by Visa, MC or AMEX only ($10.00 min.), No cash, checks or COD. Shipping & handling:
US/Can. $2.75 for one book, $1.00 for each add'l book; Int'l $5.00 for one book, $1 00 for each
add'l. Call (800) 788-6262 or (201) 933-9292, fax (201) 896-8569 or mail your orders to.

Penguin Putnam Inc.   Bill my: ❑ Visa ❑ MasterCard ❑ Amex _____ (expires)
P.O. Box 12289, Dept. B
Newark, NJ 07101-5289   Card# _____
Please allow 4-6 weeks for delivery   Signature _____
Foreign and Canadian delivery 6-8 weeks.

Bill to:

Name _____

Address _____ City _____

State/ZIP _____ Daytime Phone # _____

Ship to:

Name _____ Book Total $ _____

Address _____ Applicable Sales Tax $ _____

City _____ Postage & Handling $ _____

State/ZIP _____ Total Amount Due $ _____

This offer subject to change without notice.   Ad # 206 (8/00)

PENGUIN PUTNAM INC.
Online

Your Internet gateway to a virtual environment with
hundreds of entertaining and enlightening books
from Penguin Putnam Inc.

*While you're there, get the latest buzz on
the best authors and books around—*

Tom Clancy, Patricia Cornwell, W.E.B. Griffin,
Nora Roberts, William Gibson, Robin Cook,
Brian Jacques, Catherine Coulter, Stephen King,
Ken Follett, Terry McMillan, and many more!

**Penguin Putnam Online is located at
http://www.penguinputnam.com**

PENGUIN PUTNAM NEWS

Every month you'll get an inside look at our upcom-
ing books and new features on our site. This is an
ongoing effort to provide you with the most
up-to-date information about
our books and authors.

**Subscribe to Penguin Putnam News at
http://www.penguinputnam.com/newsletters**

From the creators of Longarm!

BUSHWHACKERS

They were the most brutal gang of cutthroats ever assembled. And during the Civil War, they sought justice outside of the law—paying back every Yankee raid with one of their own. They rode hard, shot straight, and had their way with every willin' woman west of the Mississippi. No man could stop them. No woman could resist them. And no Yankee stood a chance of living when Quantrill's Raiders rode into town...

Win and Joe Coulter became the two most wanted men in the West. And they learned just how sweet—and deadly—revenge could be...

BUSHWHACKERS by B. J. Lanagan
0-515-12102-9/$4.99
BUSHWHACKERS #2: REBEL COUNTY
0-515-12142-8/$4.99
BUSHWHACKERS#3:
THE KILLING EDGE 0-515-12177-0/$4.99
BUSHWHACKERS #4:
THE DYING TOWN 0-515-12232-7/$4.99
BUSHWHACKERS #5:
MEXICAN STANDOFF 0-515-12263-7/$4.99

BUSHWHACKERS #6:
EPITAPH 0-515-12290-4/$4.99

BUSHWHACKERS #7:
A TIME FOR KILLING 0-515-12574-1/$4.99
BUSHWHACKERS #8:
DEATH PASS 0-515-12658-6/$4.99
BUSHWHACKERS #9:
HANGMAN'S DROP 0-515-12731-0/$4.99

Prices slightly higher in Canada

Payable by Visa, MC or AMEX only ($10.00 min.), No cash, checks or COD. Shipping & handling: US/Can. $2.75 for one book, $1.00 for each add'l book; Int'l $5.00 for one book, $1.00 for each add'l. Call (800) 788-6262 or (201) 933-9292, fax (201) 896-8569 or mail your orders to:

Penguin Putnam Inc.   Bill my: ☐ Visa ☐ MasterCard ☐ Amex _____ (expires)
P.O. Box 12289, Dept. B
Newark, NJ 07101-5289   Card# _____
Please allow 4-6 weeks for delivery.
Foreign and Canadian delivery 6-8 weeks. Signature _____

Bill to:
Name _____
Address _____ City _____
State/ZIP _____ Daytime Phone # _____
Ship to:
Name _____ Book Total $ _____
Address _____ Applicable Sales Tax $ _____
City _____ Postage & Handling $ _____
State/ZIP _____ Total Amount Due $ _____

This offer subject to change without notice.   Ad #Wackers (4/01)